W9-BRO-084

"You have a lovely home."

"Indeed, yes," William replied. "I really must add a wife and children as soon as possible."

Lucy looked out the car window at the serene countryside. There was a potential wife waiting for him, wasn't there? Someone who would grace his table and manage his home to perfection. The children were another matter, but perhaps Fiona might change her mind.

She said in a wooden voice, "I hope you'll be very happy."

He said placidly, "I'm thirty-five and I've waited a long time for the right girl to come along. I know I—we shall be very happy."

There seemed to be no answer to that. William turned out of the driveway and began their journey back to England.

Betty Neels is well-known for her romances set in the Netherlands, which is hardly surprising. She married a Dutchman and spent the first twelve years of their marriage living in Holland and working as a nurse. Today she and her husband make their home in an ancient stone cottage in England's West Country, but they return to Holland often. She loves to explore tiny villages and tour privately-owned homes there in order to lend an air of authenticity to the background of her books.

Books by Betty Neels

HARLEQUIN ROMANCE
2808—TWO WEEKS TO REMEMBER
2824—THE SECRET POOL
2855—STORMY SPRINGTIME
2874—OFF WITH THE OLD LOVE
2891—THE DOUBTFUL MARRIAGE
2914—A GENTLE AWAKENING
2933—THE COURSE OF TRUE LOVE
2956—WHEN TWO PATHS MEET
3004—PARADISE FOR TWO
3024—THE FATEFUL BARGAIN
3036—NO NEED TO SAY GOOD-BYE
3053—THE CHAIN OF DESTINY
3071—HILLTOP TRYST
3084—THE CONVENIENT WIFE

Don't miss any of our special offers. Write to us at the following address for information on our newest releases.

Harlequin Reader Service
P.O. Box 1397, Buffalo, NY 14240
Canadian address: P.O. Box 603,
Fort Erie, Ont. L2A 5X3

THE GIRL
WITH GREEN EYES

Betty Neels

Harlequin Books

TORONTO • NEW YORK • LONDON
AMSTERDAM • PARIS • SYDNEY • HAMBURG
STOCKHOLM • ATHENS • TOKYO • MILAN

Original hardcover edition published in 1990
by Mills & Boon Limited

ISBN 0-373-03105-4

Harlequin Romance first edition February 1991

THE GIRL WITH GREEN EYES

Copyright © 1990 by Betty Neels.
All rights reserved. Except for use in any review, the reproduction or utilization
of this work in whole or in part in any form by any electronic, mechanical or
other means, now known or hereafter invented, including xerography,
photocopying and recording, or in any information storage or retrieval system,
is forbidden without the permission of the publisher, Harlequin Enterprises
Limited, 225 Duncan Mill Road, Don Mills, Ontario, Canada M3B 3K9.

All the characters in this book have no existence outside the imagination of
the author and have no relation whatsoever to anyone bearing the same name
or names. They are not even distantly inspired by any individual known or
unknown to the author, and all incidents are pure invention.

® are Trademarks registered in the United States Patent and Trademark Office
and in other countries.

Printed in U.S.A.

CHAPTER ONE

THE vast waiting-room, despite the cheerful yellow paint on its Victorian walls, its bright posters and even a picture or two, its small counter for tea and coffee and the play-things all scattered around, was still a depressing place. It was also a noisy one, its benches filled by mothers, babies and toddlers awaiting their turn to be seen by the consultant paediatrician. From time to time a name would be called by a plump middle-aged sister and another small patient with an evidently anxious mother would be borne away while those who were waiting re-arranged themselves hopefully.

The dark, wet day of early February was already dwindling into dusk, although it was barely four o'clock. The waiting-room was damp and chilly despite the heating, and as the rows of patients gradually lessened it seemed to become even chillier.

Presently there was only one patient left, a small fair-haired toddler, asleep curled up in the arms of the girl who held her. A pretty girl with a tip-tilted nose, a gentle mouth and large green eyes. Her abundant pale brown hair was scraped back fiercely into a top knot and she looked tired. She watched the two registrars who had been dealing with the less urgent cases come from their offices and walk away, and thought longingly of her tea. If this specialist didn't get a move on, she reflected, the child she was holding would wake and demand hers.

5

A door opened and the sister came through. 'I'm sorry, dear, that you've had to wait for so long; Dr Thurloe got held up. He'll see you now.'

The girl got up and went past her into the room beyond, hesitating inside the door. The man sitting at the desk glanced up and got to his feet, a large man and tall, with fair hair heavily sprinkled with silver and the kind of good looks to make any woman look at him twice, with a commanding nose, a wide, firm mouth and heavily lidded eyes. He smiled at her now. 'Do sit down——' his voice was slow and deep '—I am so sorry that you've had to wait for such a long time.' He sat down again and picked up the notes and doctor's letter before him; halfway through he glanced up. 'You aren't this little girl's mother?'

She had been waiting and watching him, aware of a peculiar sensation in her insides.

'Me? Oh, no. I work at the orphanage. Miranda's not very easy, but I mostly look after her; she's a darling, but she does get—well, disturbed.'

He nodded and went on reading, and she stared at his downbent head. She had frequently wondered what it would be like to fall in love, but she had never imagined that it would be quite like this—and could one fall in love with someone at first glance? Heroines in romantic novels often did, but a romantic novel was one thing, real life was something quite different, or so she had always thought. He looked up and smiled at her and her heart turned over—perhaps after all real life wasn't all that different from a romantic novel. She smiled with delight and his eyebrows rose and his glance became questioning, but since she said nothing—she was too short of breath to do that—he sat back in his chair. 'Well, now, shall we see what can be done for Miranda, Miss...?'

'Lockitt—Lucy Lockitt.'

His firm mouth quivered. '"Lost her pocket, Kitty Fisher found it..."'

'Everyone says that,' she told him seriously.

'Tiresome for you, but I suppose we all learnt nursery rhymes when we were small.' With an abrupt change of manner he went on, 'If you could put her on to the couch, I'll take a look.'

Lucy laid the still sleeping child down and the doctor came over to the couch and stood looking down at her. 'I wonder why nothing was done when hydrocephalus was first diagnosed. I see in her notes that her skull was abnormally enlarged at birth. You don't happen to know why her notes are so sparse?'

'They've been lost—that is, Matron thinks so. You see, she was abandoned when she was a few weeks old, no one knows who her parents are; they left her with the landlady of the rooms they were living in. They left some money too, so I suppose she didn't bother to see a doctor—perhaps she didn't know that Miranda wasn't quite normal. A week or two ago the landlady had to go to hospital and Miranda was taken in by neighbours who thought that there was something wrong, so they brought her to the orphanage and Dr Watts arranged for you to see her.'

Dr Thurloe bent over the toddler, who woke then and burst into tears. 'Perhaps you could undress her?' he suggested. 'Would you like Sister or one of the nurses to help you?'

'Strange faces frighten her,' said Lucy matter-of-factly, 'and I can manage, thank you.'

He was very gentle, and when he had made his general examination he said in a quiet voice, 'Take her on your lap, will you? I need to examine her head.'

It took a considerable time and he had to sit very close. A pity, thought Lucy, that for all he cares I could be one of the hospital chairs. It occurred to her then that he was probably married, with children of his own; he wasn't young, but he wasn't old either—just right, in fact. She began to puzzle out ways and means of getting to know something about him, so deeply engrossed that he had to ask her twice if she was a nurse.

'Me? Oh, no. I just go each day from nine in the morning until five o'clock in the afternoon. I do odd jobs, feeding the babies and changing them and making up cots—that sort of thing.'

He was running a gentle hand over the distended little skull. 'Was there no nurse to accompany Miranda here?'

'Well, no. You see, it's hard to get trained nurses in an orphanage—it's not very exciting, just routine. There's Matron and a deputy matron and three state enrolled nurses, and then four of us to help.'

The doctor already knew how many children there were; all the same, he asked that too.

'Between forty and fifty,' she replied, then added, 'I've been there for four years.'

He was measuring the small head with callipers, his large, well-tended hands feather-light. 'And you have never wished to train as a nurse?'

'Oh, yes, but it hasn't been possible.'

He said smoothly, 'The training does tie one down for several years. You understand what is wrong with Miranda?'

'Not precisely, only that there is too much fluid inside her skull.'

'It is a fairly rare condition—the several parts of the skull don't unite and the cerebrospinal fluid increases so that the child's head swells. There are sometimes mental symptoms, already apparent in Miranda. I should like her to be admitted here and insert a catheter in a ventricle which will drain off some of the surplus fluid.'

'Where to?'

'Possibly a pleural cavity via the jugular vein with a valve to prevent a flow-back.'

'It won't hurt her?' she asked urgently.

'No. It will need skilled attention when necessary, though.'

He straightened to his full height, towering over her. 'Will you set her to rights? I'll write to Dr Watts and arrange for her to be admitted as soon as possible.'

Lucy, arranging a nappy, just so, said thickly round the safety-pin between her teeth, 'You can cure her?'

'At least we can make life more comfortable for her. Take that pin out of your mouth, it could do a great deal of damage if you swallowed it. What transport do you have?' He glanced at the notes before him. 'Sparrow Street, isn't it? You came by ambulance?'

She shook her head, busy putting reluctant little arms into a woolly jacket. 'Taxi. I'm to get one to take us back.'

'My dear girl, it is now five o'clock and the rush hour, you might have to wait for some time. I'll arrange an ambulance,' he stretched out an arm to the telephone, 'or better still, I'll take you on my way home.'

'That's very kind of you,' said Lucy politely, 'but it wouldn't do at all, you know. For one thing the orphanage is in Willoughby Street and that's even more East End than here, and for another, I'm sure consultants don't make a habit of giving lifts to their patients—though perhaps you do if they're private...'

The doctor sat back in his chair and looked her over. 'I am aware of where the orphanage is and I give lifts to anyone I wish to. You have a poor opinion of consultants... We are, I should suppose, exactly like anyone else.'

'Oh, I'm sure you are,' said Lucy kindly, 'only much cleverer, of course.'

His heavy eyelids lifted, revealing a pair of very blue eyes. 'A debatable point,' he observed. 'And now if you will go to the front entrance I will meet you there in a few minutes.'

He spoke quietly and she did as he asked, because she had to admit to herself that he had that kind of voice and she was tired. Miranda had gone to sleep again, but once she woke she would want her tea and her cot and would fly into a storm of tears; to be driven back to the orphanage would be a relief. She was already late and it would be another half-hour or more before she was home. She sat on a bench facing the door so that she would see the doctor when he came, but he came unnoticed from one of the corridors at the back of the entrance hall. He paused before he reached her and gave her a long look; she was pretty enough to warrant it, and seen in profile her nose had a most appealing tilt... He spoke as he reached her. 'The car's just outside. It will be better if you carry her, I think; it wouldn't do to wake her.'

They crossed the hall and he held the door for her and went ahead to open the door of the dark grey Rolls-

Royce outside. She got in carefully and he fastened her safety-belt without disturbing the child, and then got in beside her, drove out of the forecourt and joined the stream of traffic in the street.

Lucy waited until they stopped in a traffic jam. 'You said Sparrow Street, and it is, of course, only the staff and children use the Willoughby Street entrance.'

'I see—and who uses the Sparrow Street door?' He edged the car forward a few yards and turned to look at her.

'Oh, the committee and visiting doctors and the governors—you know, important people.'

'I should have thought that in an orphanage the orphans were the important people.'

'They are. They're awfully well looked after.' She lapsed into silence as the big car slid smoothly ahead and presently stopped in Willoughby Street. The doctor got out and opened her door for her and she got out carefully. 'Thank you very much for the lift, it was kind of you.' She smiled up into his impassive face.

'I'm coming in with you, I want to see the matron. Where do you live?'

'Me? In Chelsea.'

'I pass it on my way home. I'll drop you off.'

'I'll be at least fifteen minutes...'

'So shall I.' They had gone inside and he indicated the row of chairs lined up against the wall of the small reception room. 'Wait here, will you?'

He nodded to the nurse who came to meet them and walked off, leaving Lucy to follow her to the back of the building where the toddlers had their cots and where the sister-in-charge was waiting. It was all of fifteen minutes by the time Lucy had explained everything, handed over the now wakeful Miranda, and said goodnight.

'Thanks for staying on over your time,' Sister said. 'I'll make it up to you some time.' She smiled nicely because Lucy was a good worker and didn't grumble at the unending task of keeping the toddlers clean and fed and happy. We could do with a few more like her, she thought, watching Lucy's slender shape disappearing down the corridor.

There was no sign of the doctor when Lucy got back to the reception-room. Perhaps she had been too long and he had gone without her, and she could hardly blame him for that—he had probably had a long and tiring day and was just as anxious to get home as she was. All the same, she sat down on one of the hard wooden chairs; there was no one else there, or she could have asked...

He came five minutes later, calm and unhurried, smiling genially, and accompanied by the matron. Lucy got to her feet and, rather to her surprise, was thanked for her afternoon's duties; it was by no means an uncommon thing for her to take children to hospital to be examined, and she was surprised that anyone had found it necessary to thank her. She muttered politely, added a goodnight and followed the doctor out to his car.

'Exactly where do you live?' he enquired of her as he settled himself beside her.

She mentioned a quiet road, one of those leading away from the Embankment, and added, 'It is very kind of you. I hope it's not taking you out of your way?'

'I live in Chiswick. Do you share a flat?' The question was casual.

'Me? No. I live with my parents...'

'Of course, now I remember—is your father an archaeologist, *the* Gregory Lockitt?' And when she murmured that he was, 'I met your parents some time ago at a dinner party. They were just back from the Andes.'

'That's right,' she agreed composedly, 'they travel a good deal.'

'But you prefer your orphanage?' His voice was kindly impersonal.

'Yes.' She didn't add to that, to explain that it was a job she had found for herself and taken on with the good humoured tolerance of her parents. She had been a disappointment to them, she knew that, although they had never actually said so; her elder sister, with a university degree and distinguished good looks, was personal assistant to the director of a City firm, and her younger sister, equally good-looking and chic with it, worked in one of the art galleries—moreover she was engaged to a young executive who was rising through his financial world with the ruthless intention of reaching the top before anyone else. Only Lucy, the middle sister and overshadowed by them both, had failed to be a success. There was no question but that they all loved her with an easygoing tolerance, but there was also no question that she had failed to live up to the family's high standards. She was capable, sensible and practical and not in the least clever, and despite her gentle prettiness she was a shy girl. At twenty-five, she knew that her mother was beginning to despair of her marrying.

Dr Thurloe stopped the car before her home and got out to open her door, and she thanked him again. Pauline and Imogen would have known exactly what to say to make him interested enough to suggest meeting again, but she had no idea; the only thought in her head was that she wasn't likely to see him again, and that almost broke her heart. She stared up into his face, learning it by heart, knowing that she would never forget it, still bemused by the surprise of loving him.

His quiet, 'A pleasure, enjoy your evening, Miss Lockitt,' brought her to her senses again, and she bade him a hasty goodnight and thumped the door knocker. He waited by his car until Alice, the housekeeper, opened the door, and then he got into the car and drove away. Perhaps I should have asked him in, reflected Lucy uneasily as she said hello to Alice.

'And who was that now?' asked Alice. 'Nice car too. Got yourself a young man, love?'

Lucy shook her head. 'Just a lift home. Is everyone in, Alice?'

'In the drawing-room and 'is nibs with them.' She gave Lucy a motherly pat. 'Best go and tidy yerself, love— they're having drinks...'

Lucy went slowly upstairs to her room, showered and got into a wool dress, brushed out her hair and did her face. She knew her mother disliked her wearing the clothes she had worn at the orphanage, even though they were covered by an overall and a plastic apron. She didn't hurry—there would just be time for a drink before dinner, and that meant that she wouldn't have to listen to Cyril, Pauline's fiancé, prosing about stocks and shares for too long. She went slowly downstairs, wondering if her sister really loved him or whether she was merely carried away at the prospect of being the wife of a successful businessman, with a flat in town, a nice little cottage in the country, two cars and enough money to allow her to dress well and entertain lavishly. In Lucy's opinion, none of these was a good reason for marrying him.

She found them all sitting round the fire in the drawing-room and her mother looked round to say, 'There you are, darling. Have the orphans been trying? You're so late...'

Lucy took the drink her father had handed her and she sat down beside him. 'I took one of them to be seen by a specialist at the City Royal; it took rather a long time.' She didn't say any more, for they weren't interested—although they always asked her about her day, they didn't listen to her reply. And indeed, she admitted to herself, it made dull listening compared with Pauline's witty accounts of the people who had called in to the art gallery, and Imogen's amusing little titbits of news about the important people she met so often. She sipped her sherry and listened to Cyril clearing his throat preparatory to addressing them. He never just talked, she thought; he either gave a potted lecture, or gave them his opinion about some matter with the air of a man who believed that no one else was clever enough to do so. She swallowed her sherry in a gulp and listened to his diatribe about the National Health Service. She didn't hear a word; she was thinking about Dr Thurloe.

Later, as Lucy said goodnight to her mother, that lady observed lightly, 'You were very quiet this evening, darling—quieter than usual. Is this little job of yours too much for you, do you suppose?'

Lucy wondered if her mother had any idea of what her little job entailed, but she didn't say so. 'Oh, no, Mother.' She spoke briskly. 'It's really easy...'

'Oh, good—it doesn't bore you?'

'Not in the least.' How could she ever explain to her mother that the orphans were never boring? Tiresome, infuriating, lovable and exhausting, but never boring. 'I only help around, you know.'

Her mother offered a cheek for a goodnight kiss. 'Well, as long as you're happy, darling. I do wish you could meet some nice man...'

But I have, thought Lucy, and a lot of good it's done me. She said 'Goodnight, Mother dear...'

'Goodnight, Lucy. Don't forget we are all going to the Walters' for dinner tomorrow evening, so don't be late home, and wear something pretty.'

Lucy went to bed and forgot all about the dinner party; she was going over, syllable by syllable, every word which Dr Thurloe had uttered.

She got home in good time the next evening. The day had been busy and she felt the worse for wear, so it was a relief to find that her sisters were in their rooms dressing and her parents were still out. She drank the tea Alice had just made, gobbled a slice of toast and went to her room to get ready for the party.

The Walters were old friends of her parents, recently retired from the diplomatic service, and Lucy and her sisters had known them since they were small girls; the friendship was close enough for frequent invitations to their dinner parties. Lucy burrowed through her wardrobe, deciding what to wear. She had a nice taste in dress, although she wasn't a slavish follower of fashion, and the green dress she finally hauled out was simple in style with a long, full skirt, long, tight sleeves and a round, low neckline. She ran a bath and then lay in it, daydreaming about Dr Thurloe, quite forgetting the time, so that she had to dress in a tearing hurry, brush out her hair and dash on powder and lipstick without much thought to her appearance. Everyone was in the hall waiting for her as she ran downstairs and her mother said tolerantly, 'Darling, you're wearing that green dress again. Surely it's time you had something new?'

'You'd better come with me on your next free day,' said Imogen. 'I know just the shop for you—there was a gorgeous pink suit in the window, just right for you.'

Lucy forbore from saying that she didn't look nice in pink, only if it were very pale pink like almond blossom. 'Sorry if I've kept you all waiting. Pauline, you and Imogen look stunning enough for the lot of us.'

Pauline patted her on the shoulder. 'You could look stunning too,' she pointed out, 'if you took the trouble.'

It was pointless to remind her sister that the orphans didn't mind whether she looked stunning or not. She followed her father out to the car and squashed into the back with her sisters.

The Walters gave rather grand dinner parties; they had many friends and they enjoyed entertaining. The Lockitts found that there were half a dozen guests already there, and Mrs Walter, welcoming them warmly, observed that there were only two more expected. 'That charming Mrs Seymour,' she observed, 'so handsome, and I dare say very lonely now that she is widowed, and I don't know if you've met——' She broke off, smiling towards the door, 'Here he is, anyway. William, how delightful that you could come! I was just saying...perhaps you know Mrs Lockitt?'

Imogen and Pauline had gone to speak to Mr Walter; only Lucy was with her mother. She watched Dr Thurloe, the very epitome of the well-dressed man, walk towards his hostess, her gentle mouth slightly open, her cheeks pinkening with surprise and delight. Here he was again, fallen as it were into her lap, and on his own too, so perhaps he wasn't married or even engaged.

He greeted his hostess, shook hands with Lucy's mother, and when Mrs Walter would have introduced Lucy he forestalled her with a pleasant, 'Oh, but we have already met—during working hours...'

He smiled down at Lucy, who beamed back at him, regretting at the same time that she had worn the green, by no means her prettiest dress. She regretted it even more as the door was opened again and Mrs Seymour swept in. A splendid blonde, exquisitely dressed and possessed of a haughty manner and good looks, she greeted Mrs Walter with a kiss on one cheek, bade Mrs Lockitt a charming good evening, smiled perfunctorily at Lucy, and turned to the doctor. 'William!' she exclaimed. 'I had no idea that you would be here—I had to take a taxi. If I'd known you could have picked me up.' She smiled sweetly and Lucy ground silent teeth. 'But you shall drive me home—you will, won't you?'

'Delighted, Fiona.'

She put a hand on his sleeve and said brightly, 'Oh, there is Tim Wetherby, I must speak to him—you know him, of course...'

It seemed that Dr Thurloe did. The pair of them strolled away and, since Mrs Walter had turned aside to talk to one of the guests, Lucy was left standing by her mother.

Mrs Lockitt gave her an exasperated glance. 'I want to talk to Mr Walter before we go into dinner. Do exert yourself, darling, and go and chat with someone—it is such a pity that you're so shy...'

A remark which made Lucy even more so. But, obedient to her mother's suggestion, she joined a group of people she knew and made the kind of conversation expected of her while managing to keep an eye on the doctor. That he and Fiona Seymour knew each other well was obvious, but Lucy had already decided that Fiona was not at all the kind of girl he should marry—he needed a wife who would listen to him when he got back from his work each day, someone who liked children, someone who understood how tiresome they could be and how lovable and how ill... Lucy nodded her head gently, seeing herself as that wife. She wasn't sure how she was going to set about it, but she would find a way.

'You're not listening to a word I'm saying,' remarked the young man who had been talking for a few minutes. When she apologised, everyone laughed—nicely, because they liked her—and someone said, 'Lucy's thinking about her orphans.' Her job was a mild joke among those she knew and there was no malice in the remark. She smiled at the speaker as they went in to dinner.

She sat between the Walters' rather solemn elder son and a young man attached to one of the foreign embassies, now home on leave, and she dutifully lent an attentive ear first to Joe Walter's explaining rather prosily about computers, and then to her neighbour on the other side, who was anxious to tell her what a splendid time he was having in his far-flung post. With an effort she smiled and nodded and said all the right things, and the doctor, from the other side of the table, thought how restful she was and how very pretty. She looked different, of course, dressed in that green thing and with her hair curling almost to her shoulders. She was sensible too, when it came to handling small children. He bent a bland listening face towards his dinner companion while he allowed the nucleus of a plan to take shape in his sagacious mind.

People sat around talking after dinner, and beyond a few passing remarks Lucy saw nothing of the doctor. Since she left with her family before he did, she had no chance to see him and Fiona Seymour leave together. She told herself stoutly that it didn't matter one bit, one day she would marry him, only she couldn't leave it too long, for she was twenty-five already. She was immensely cheered by the thought that Mrs Seymour, however well made-up she was, couldn't disguise the fact that she wouldn't see thirty again.

Back home, all of them in the kitchen, drinking hot milk before bed, her mother remarked, 'What a nice man William Thurloe is, so good-looking and clever and not an ounce of conceit in him.'

'We had quite a long chat,' said Imogen complacently.

'But Fiona Seymour has got her talons into him,' said Pauline. She added, 'He must be all of thirty-five—she'd make him a very suitable wife.'

'Why?' asked Lucy quietly.

Both sisters turned to look at her. 'She's what is known as a handsome woman, intelligent and always well dressed,' they chorused kindly, 'and she would look just right sitting opposite him at the dinner table. A splendid hostess...'

'But she can't be a hostess all the time—I mean, what about looking after the children, and seeing that he gets a good meal when he comes home late, and gets enough sleep...?'

Her family stared at her. 'Why, Lucy,' said her mother, 'you sound,' she paused, seeking a word, 'concerned.'

Lucy finished her milk and put the mug in the sink. 'I just think that Fiona Seymour isn't the wife for him. He was the specialist I took Miranda to see yesterday; he likes children and somehow I don't think she does.' She kissed her mother and father, nodded goodnight to her sisters and went up to her room. She had said more than she had intended to say, which had been silly of her. The doctor's future was nothing to her; she would probably meet him from time to time at some mutual friend's house, and he would greet her politely and go and talk to someone else, forgetting her at once.

It was raining dismally when she left home the next morning. The orphanage looked bleaker than ever as she got off her bus, although once inside it became more cheerful with its bright painted walls and colourful curtains. All the same, the morning dragged with its unending round of chores. She was ministering to a vomiting four-year-old when Sister came to find her. 'Matron wants you in the office, Lucy. You'd better go at once.'

Lucy handed over the small child, took off her apron and made her way to the office on the first floor.

Matron was quite young and well liked. 'Sit down, Lucy,' she invited. 'I've a favour to ask of you. Miranda has to go off into hospital in two days' time. Dr Thurloe has asked if you would be allowed to go with her—it's important that she is not too disturbed, and she responds to you. You would have to live at the City Royal for a few days—she would be in a room off the children's ward and you would have a room next to hers. You would be relieved for meals and off-duty, but it might be necessary for you to get up at night if she is very disturbed.' She smiled. 'And we both know what that's like.'

'Yes, of course I'll go, Matron.' Lucy smiled too; she would see Dr Thurloe again after all, and perhaps she would be able to say something witty or clever and get his attention—not just polite attention, but real interest... 'When exactly are we to go?'

'Have a day off tomorrow and report here at eight o'clock on the day after. I believe Dr Thurloe means to insert the tube later in the day, and I must warn you that you may have a difficult night afterwards. It depends on her reactions as to how long she stays there. You'll be free?'

'Oh, yes, Matron—for as long as you want me to be with Miranda.'

'Good, that's settled, then. I won't keep you longer.'

The day had suddenly become perfect; the children were little angels, and the hours sped away in a flurry of tasks which were no longer boring or tiresome. Lucy changed nappies, cleaned up messes, fed protesting toddlers and dreamt of the days ahead, days in which she would become the object of admiration—Dr Thurloe's admiration—because of some skilful act on her part— saving Miranda's life by her quick thinking, rescuing a ward full of children by her bravery in case of fire... a bomb outrage... burst pipes...? It didn't really matter what it was as long as it caused him to notice her and then fall in love with her.

She finished at last and went off duty and home. It was still raining, and as she hurried from the bus-stop the steady downpour brought her to her usual senses. She laughed out loud so that an elderly couple passing

looked at her with suspicion. 'No more useless daydreaming,' she told herself briskly. 'You're too old for
that anyway, but that doesn't mean that you aren't going
to marry him some day.'

It was nice to be home for a day. She pottered around,
helping her mother with the flowers, sorting out the
sheets of scrawled writing which flowed from her father's
pen as he worked at the lengthy task of putting together
notes for the book he intended to write. At the end of
the day she packed the bag that she would need while
she was in hospital, washed her hair, did her nails and
inspected her pretty face for the first wrinkles and lines.
She couldn't find any.

She and Miranda were fetched from the orphanage by
ambulance the next morning, and to everyone's relief
the child slept quietly in Lucy's arms. It wasn't until
they were in the room where she was to stay that she
woke and, sensing something out of the ordinary, began
to cry.

Lucy sat down, still in her outdoor things, and set
about the task of quieting Miranda. She had just suc-
ceeded when Dr Thurloe came in.

His 'Good morning, Lucy,' was quietly spoken and
uttered with impersonal courtesy before he began giving
the ward sister his instructions, and presently Miranda,
still snivelling a bit, was given an injection and carried
away to Theatre, leaving Lucy free to unpack her bag
in the adjoining room and envelop her nicely curved
person in the voluminous overall she had been told that
she must wear. Her duties, as far as she could make out,
were light enough—certainly no worse than they were at
the orphanage. The only difference was that they would
extend for a much longer period each day, and quite

possibly each night too. A small price to pay for seeing the doctor from time to time, and on his own ground too.

She drank the coffee that one of the nurses brought her; the nurse was a nice girl, but faintly condescending. 'Why don't you train as a nurse?' she asked.

'I'm not clever,' observed Lucy, 'but I like children.' She might have added that she had no need to earn her living, and that her mother and father found it difficult to understand as well as faintly amusing that she should spend her days feeding babies and toddlers and everlastingly clearing up their mess, only it didn't enter her head to do so.

'How long will it take?' she wanted to know, and was treated to a lengthy description of exactly what Dr Thurloe was doing. She didn't understand half of it, but it was nice to talk about him. 'I thought he was a physician,' she ventured.

The nurse gave her an impatient look. 'Well, of course he is, but he does this kind of surgery too. He's a paediatrician—that's a children's doctor.'

Lucy, who had looked all that up in her father's study, already knew that, but she expressed suitable gratitude for being told, and when her companion said importantly that she must return to the ward and continue what sounded like a mountain of tasks, she thanked her for her company and settled herself down to wait. It wouldn't be too long.

Miranda returned ten minutes later, borne in the arms of Theatre Sister and already rousing from the anaesthetic. There was just time for her to be settled in Lucy's arms before she opened her eyes, and then her small mouth was ready to let out an enraged yell.

'Hello, love,' said Lucy in her gentle voice, and Miranda smiled instead.

'Lucy,' she mumbled contentedly, and closed her eyes and her mouth too.

Dr Thurloe, standing silently behind her, nodded his handsome head. He had been right to follow his instinctive wish to have Lucy there; it would make things a good deal easier on the ward, and besides, she looked nice sitting there in that oversized overall. He had a sudden jumble of ridiculous thoughts run through his clever head; nurseries, rice pudding, children shouting and laughing, and small figures pattering to and fro... He frowned. Fiona had told him laughingly only the other day that he saw enough children without needing any of his own. 'What you need,' she had told him in her charming way, 'is a quiet house to come home to, pleasant evenings with friends, and someone to talk to at the end of the day without any interruptions.' She had made it sound very inviting and, because he had been very tired then, he had more or less agreed with her, but now he realised that that wasn't what he wanted. He wasn't sure what he did want, and anyway, it was hardly the time to worry about it now. He went to bend over his small patient, taking no notice of Lucy, then he gave more instructions to his ward sister and went away.

CHAPTER TWO

THE day seemed very long to Lucy. She was relieved for her meals, but Miranda, now fully awake, became restless towards the evening, and the only way to placate her was for Lucy to take her on her lap and murmur the moppet's favourite nursery rhymes over and over again in her gentle voice. But eventually Miranda slept, and Lucy was able to tuck her into her cot and, with a nurse in her place, go to the canteen for her supper. The nurses there were casually kind, showing her where to get her meal and where she might sit, but beyond a few smiles and hellos she was ignored while they discussed their work on the wards, their boyfriends and their lack of money. She ate her supper quickly and slipped away unnoticed, back to the austere little room where Miranda was. The ward sister was there conning the chart.

'Had your supper? Good. Night Sister will be along in about an hour. I think it might be a good idea if you had a bath and got ready for bed while I can spare a nurse to sit here—that will mean that if Miranda wakes up later and is difficult you'll be available. Go to bed once Sister's been—but you do know you may have to get up in the night? I don't think there will be a nurse to spare to attend the child; we're rather busy...'

She nodded and smiled and went away, and Lucy set about getting ready for bed in her own small room, leaving the door open in case Miranda woke and the nurse couldn't placate her.

But the child slept on and Lucy bathed in peace, brushed her hair, got into a dressing-gown and padded back to take the nurse's place.

The nurse yawned. 'She hasn't moved,' she told Lucy. 'She looks like a cherub, doesn't she? If it weren't for that outsized head...' She glanced at her watch. 'I'm off duty, thank heaven; it's been a long day. See you in the morning.'

Lucy sat down. Miranda was sleeping peacefully, and her pulse, which Lucy had been shown how to take and record, was exactly as it should be. Lucy studied the chart and started to read up the notes behind it. The small operation had been written up in red ink in an almost unreadable scrawl and initialled W.T., and she puzzled it out with patience. Dr Thurloe might be an excellent paediatrician, but his writing appeared to be appalling. She smiled, pleased that she knew something about him, and then she sat quietly thinking about him until Night Sister, a small brisk woman, came into the room. She checked the valve, looked at the chart and asked, 'You know what you're looking for, Miss Lockitt? Slow pulse, vomiting, headache—not that Miranda will be able to tell you that... But if you're worried, or even doubtful, ring the bell at once. I'll be back later on, and if I can't come then my junior night sister will. I should go to bed if I were you. Her pulse is steady and she's sleeping, but I depend on you to see to her during the night.'

She went away as quietly as she had come, and Lucy did as she had been told and got into the narrow, cold bed in the adjoining room. She got up again in a few minutes and put on her dressing-gown again, and then tucked her cold feet into its cosy folds and rolled into a tight ball, and dozed off.

It was only a little after an hour later when Miranda's first restless whimpers woke her. She was out of bed in a flash and bending over the cot. Miranda was awake and cross, but her pulse seemed all right. Lucy picked her up carefully and sat down with her on her lap, gave her a drink and began the one-sided conversation which the toddler seemed to enjoy. Miranda stopped grizzling and presently began a conversation of her own, although when Lucy stopped talking her small face creased into infantile rage again, so that Lucy hurried into the Three Bears, growling gently so that Miranda chuckled. 'And Father Bear blew on his porridge to cool it,' said Lucy, and blew, to stop and draw a quick breath because Dr Thurloe had come silently into the room and was watching her. He had someone with him, a pretty, dark girl in sister's uniform, and it was to her that he spoke. 'You see, Marian, how well my plan has worked? With Miss Lucy Lockitt's co-operation we shall have Miranda greatly improved in no time.'

He nodded, smiling faintly at Lucy. 'Has she been very restless?'

'No, only for the last twenty minutes or so. She began to cry, but I think she'll settle down again.' She went red at his look; she had no business telling a specialist something he must already know for himself.

'I'll take a look while I'm here. Can you sit her up a little on your knee?'

He bent over her to examine Miranda and Lucy studied the top of his head; he had a lot of hair, a pleasing mixture of fairness and silver cut short by a master hand.

He straightened up and spoke to the sister. 'I think something to settle her, don't you, Marian?' He glanced at the thin gold watch on his wrist. 'Let's see, it's getting on for eleven o'clock.' He glanced at Lucy. 'A few hours of sleep will do you both good...' He took the chart from the sister's hand and wrote. 'That should see to it.' He walked to the door. 'Go to bed, Miss Lockitt; Sister will see that someone wakes you before Miranda rouses. Goodnight.'

He had gone before she could reply. She waited until the sister came back with an injection and then sat soothing Miranda until she dozed off and she was able to tuck her up in her cot once more. She wasn't very happy about going back to bed, but she was sure that Dr Thurloe wouldn't have suggested it if he hadn't been quite convinced that Miranda would sleep quietly for a few hours. So she got back into bed again and presently fell asleep, to wake very early in the morning and go and take a look at Miranda, who was still sleeping peacefully. Lucy took her pulse and was relieved to find that it was just what it was supposed to be. She was dressed and tied into her ample overall long before a nurse poked her head round the door. 'Oh, good, you're up already. I'll bring you a cup of tea just as soon as I've got the time. If she wakes can you wash her and pot her?'

Lucy nodded. 'Oh, yes. I expect I'll need clean sheets and another nightie.'

'In that cupboard in the corner, and there's a plastic bag where you can put the stuff that needs washing...'

The nurse's head disappeared to be replaced almost at once by the bulk of Dr Thurloe, immaculate and looking as though he had had ten hours' sleep. He was alone this time and his 'good morning' was friendly, so that Lucy regretted that she hadn't bothered to powder her nose or put on lipstick.

'Had a good night? You're up early.'

'So are you,' observed Lucy, and wished she hadn't said it; she must remember that they weren't at a dinner party but in hospital, where he was someone important and she wasn't of any account, especially in the bunchy garment she was wearing. And she felt worse because he didn't answer her, only bent over the cot.

'We'll have a look,' he said with impersonal politeness, and waited expectantly.

Lucy took down the cot side. She said in her sensible way, 'She's wet—I didn't like to change her until I'd seen Sister. Do you mind?'

The look he gave her was amused and kind too. 'I dare say I've dealt with more wet infants than you've had hot dinners. No, I don't mind! I'm glad she's had a good night. I don't intend to give her anything today though, and you may have your work cut out keeping her happy.'

He was halfway through his examination when the junior night sister came in. She said sharply, 'I'm sorry, sir, I didn't know you were here.' And then to Lucy. 'You should have rung the bell, Miss Lockitt.'

'My fault,' said the doctor smoothly, 'I told her not to bother.' Which was kind of him, reflected Lucy, listening to him giving the night sister his instructions. 'And I'll be in some time during the day. I think Miranda will be all right, but we must look out for mental disturbance—there may be a deficiency...'

Lucy couldn't understand everything he was saying, but she presumed it wasn't necessary; she was there to keep Miranda quiet and happy until she was deemed fit to return to the orphanage. She supposed that would be in a couple of days' time and that she would be told in due course. The doctor strolled to the door with the junior night sister beside him. As he went out of the room, he said over his shoulder, 'Thank you, Miss Lockitt. Be sure and let someone know if you're anxious about anything, never mind how trivial it may seem.'

Lucy watched him go, wishing with her whole heart that she were the junior night sister, not only on good terms with him, but able to understand what he was talking about and give the right answers. Not for the first time she wished fervently that she were clever and not just practical and sensible.

There was no point in dwelling upon that; Miranda was showing signs of waking up, and she fetched clean linen from the cupboard and ran warm water into the deep sink in one corner of the room. She was very grateful when the nurse brought her a cup of tea, for the next half-hour was busy and noisy: Miranda was fretful and screamed her annoyance at the top of her voice. It was nothing new, and Lucy did all that was necessary, talking in her quiet voice all the while. When the ward sister came on duty and poked her head round the door with a 'Can you cope alone?' Lucy said placidly that she was quite all right, thank you, and the head disappeared without another word. She had Miranda tucked up in bed by the time a nurse came with the toddler's breakfast. 'Ring when she's had it,' she advised, 'and someone will relieve you while you go to the canteen.' She grinned widely. 'I bet you're ready for breakfast. Did you get a cup of tea?'

'Yes, thanks. Are you very busy?'

The nurse cast her eyes to heaven. 'You can say that again.' She darted off leaving Lucy to feed Miranda, who, clean and smiling again, was more than pleased to eat her breakfast.

The same nurse came back when Lucy rang the bell. 'Half an hour,' she warned. 'We've got theatre cases this morning, so it's all go. Someone will bring you coffee, though, and you'll get time for your dinner. I don't know about off-duty, I expect that Sister will tell you.'

Lucy went thankfully to the canteen; she was hungry, and besides, it was nice to have a change of scene. She was fond of Miranda and she saw a lot of her at the orphanage, but all the same she could see that her patience and good temper were going to be tried for the next day or two.

There weren't many people in the canteen. She took her tray to a table by a window and ate with her eye on the clock, and then hurried back to find Miranda sobbing and refusing to be comforted. It took a little while to soothe her again, but presently the little girl fell asleep and Lucy was free to walk round the little room and look out of the window. The hospital forecourt was below. She watched Dr Thurloe's car come to a dignified halt in the consultants' car park, and then studied him as he got out and crossed to the hospital entrance. He walked fast, but halfway there he paused and looked up to the window where she stood. There wasn't time to draw back; she stood there while he looked and presently went on his way.

She was in the canteen having her dinner when he came to see Miranda again, and that evening it was his registrar who paid a visit. And in the morning when he came with the ward sister his good morning to Lucy was pleasant but cool, and anything he had to say was said to the sister.

Miranda was to go back to the orphanage the next day; everything was going well and the matron there would know how to deal with any emergency. Miranda was to come to his next out-patients' clinic in two weeks' time. He paused to thank Lucy as he went away. She was watching him go with regret; at the same time her wish to marry him had never been so strong.

She took Miranda back the next day without having seen him again. He was in the hospital; his car was parked in the forecourt. She glimpsed it as she got into the ambulance which was to take them to the orphanage. She consoled herself with the thought that she would be taking Miranda to his clinic in two weeks' time. In the meantime she might be able to think of something to attract his attention. A different hairstyle? Different make-up? A striking outfit? Better still, a few amusing, witty remarks... She occupied her brief ride trying to think of them.

It was early afternoon by the time she had handed over Miranda and reported to Matron, to be told that, since she had had almost no time off in the hospital, she was to go home at once and not return to the orphanage until the day following the next.

'You enjoyed your stay at the City Royal?'

'Yes, thank you. I didn't have anything much to do, just keep Miranda happy and see that she ate her food. She was very good.'

'She slept?'

'Oh, quite a bit. I got up once or twice during the night, but she soon settled.'

'Good. Dr Thurloe seemed to be pleased with the arrangement; it took a good deal of the work off the nurses' shoulders. Miranda seems to need a lot of attention, but he thinks that she will improve fairly rapidly.'

'That's good. What will happen to her, Matron? I mean when she's older and more—more normal?'

'Well, as to that, we must wait and see. But she will always have a home here, you know. Now do go home, you must be tired.'

It was still early afternoon and only Alice was at home when Lucy let herself in. 'A nice cup of tea and a sandwich or two,' said Alice comfortably. 'You look tired, love. Your mother and father are at the Victoria and Albert. Someone there wanted your pa to see some old rocks that someone had sent from Africa—or was it the Andes? One of those foreign places, anyway. They won't be back until after tea. Imogen's working late and Pauline's going out to dinner with her fiancé.' She sniffed. 'You go and change and I'll have a snack for you in ten minutes.'

So Lucy went to her room, unpacked her few things, had a shower, washed her hair and wandered downstairs with her head in a towel and wearing a dressing-gown. Her mother wouldn't have approved, but since the house was empty except for herself and Alice she couldn't see that it mattered. Alice had made a pot of tea and cut a plateful of sandwiches and Lucy sat down at the kitchen table to eat them. Somehow she had missed dinner at the hospital, what with feeding Miranda and getting her ready to go back to the orphanage, and the nurses on the ward being in short supply since they took it in turns to go to the canteen. She lifted the edge of a sandwich and saw with satisfaction that it was generously filled with chopped egg and cress. She wolfed it down delicately, poured tea and invited Alice to have a cup.

'Not me, love,' said Alice. ''Ad me lunch not an hour back. You eat that lot and have a nice rest before your mother and father come home.'

Lucy polished off the egg and cress and started on the ham. The kitchen was pleasantly warm and cheerful. It was a semi-basement room, for the house had been built at the turn of the century, a late Victorian gentleman's residence with ornate brickwork and large rooms. It had been Lucy's home for as long as she could remember, and although her mother often expressed a wish for a house in the country nothing ever came of it, for the Chelsea house was convenient for her father's headquarters; he still travelled widely, taking her mother with him, and when they were at home he worked for various museums and he lectured a good deal. Lucy, a sensible girl not given to wanting things she couldn't have, accepted her life cheerfully, aware that she didn't quite fit in with her family and that she was a source of mild disappointment, to her mother at least, even though she was loved. Until now she had been quite prepared to go on working at the orphanage with the hope at the back of her mind that one day she would meet a man who might want to marry her. So far she hadn't met anyone whom she would want to marry—that was, until she'd met Dr Thurloe. An event which incited her to do something about it. She took another sandwich and bit into it. Clothes, she thought, new clothes—she had plenty, but a few more might help—and then she might try and discover mutual friends—the Walters, of course, for a

start, and there must be others. Her parents knew any
number of people, it would be a process of elimination.
But first the new clothes, so that if and when they met
again she would be able to compete with Fiona Seymour.

The front door bell, one of a row of old-fashioned
bells along the kitchen wall, jangled and Alice put down
the plates that she was stacking.

'Postman?' asked Lucy. 'He's late...'

'I'd best go, I suppose,' grumbled Alice, and went out
of the kitchen, shutting the door after her as she went
up the short flight of stairs to the hall.

Lucy sat back, a second cup of tea in her hand. There
was one sandwich left; it was a pity to leave it. She took
it off the plate and bit into it. The door behind her
opened and she said, 'Was it the postman?' and turned
round as she took another bite.

Alice had returned, but not alone. Dr Thurloe was
with her, looking completely at home, elegant as always
and smiling faintly.

'Gracious heavens!' Lucy spoke rather thickly because of the sandwich. 'Whatever are you doing here?'
She put an agitated hand up to the towel. 'I've just
washed my hair...'

She frowned heavily, all her plans knocked edgeways;
instead of sporting an elegant outfit and a tidy head of
hair, here she was looking just about as awful as she
possibly could. She turned the frown on Alice and the
doctor spoke.

'Don't be annoyed with your housekeeper, I told her
that you wouldn't mind. You don't, do you? After all,
I've seen you in a dressing-gown at the hospital.' He
sounded kind and friendly and the smile held charm.

Lucy smiled back. 'Is it something important? Would you like a cup of tea?'

'Indeed I would.'

Alice gave a small sound which might have been a chuckle and pulled out a chair. 'The kettle's on the boil,' she informed him, 'and I've as nice a bit of Madeira cake as you'll taste anywhere, though I says it that oughtn't, being me own baking.'

'I'm partial to Madeira cake, and what a pleasant kitchen you have.'

He sat down opposite Lucy and eyed the towel. 'Do you know, all the girls I know go to the hairdresser every few days; I can't remember when I last saw a young woman washing her own hair.' He studied Lucy thoughtfully. 'Will it take long to dry?'

'No. It's almost dry now.' She poured him a cup of tea from the fresh pot Alice had put on the table. 'Is it something to do with Miranda? She's not ill...?'

'No, she's doing nicely. I wondered if we might go somewhere this evening and have dinner; I'm sure you would like to know the details of her treatment, and there really was no time at the City Royal to say much.'

He ate some cake and watched her, amused at her hesitation.

'Well,' said Lucy, 'Mother and Father——' She was interrupted by the telephone's ringing, and Alice answered it. She listened for a moment, said, 'Yes, ma'am' twice and then hung up. 'Yer ma and pa,' she told Lucy. 'They're going on to Professor Schinkel's house for dinner.' She added, 'I expect your ma thought you weren't home today.'

The look on Lucy's face made the doctor say quickly, 'Now isn't that providential, you will be free to dine with me, then?' That settled, he took another piece of cake and passed his cup for more tea. 'Your sisters won't mind?'

'They're both out too.'

'Then may I call for you this evening? Half-past seven or thereabouts? Somewhere fairly quiet? Boulestin's, perhaps?'

'That sounds very nice,' said Lucy, 'but only if you can spare the time...'

He looked as though he was going to laugh, but said gravely, 'As far as I know there will be no calls upon me until tomorrow morning at nine o'clock.' He got to his feet. 'Until half-past seven. I look forward to it.'

Alice showed him out and came bustling back. 'There now, what a nice gentleman, to be sure. Take that towel off and I'll dry that hair. What will you wear?' She began to rub vigorously. 'That's a posh restaurant...'

'Those sandals I got from Rayne's and haven't worn— and I'll leave my hair loose...'

'All right as far as it goes, but what about a dress? Sandals and hair aren't enough.'

'That silver-grey satin, you know, the one with the calf-length skirt and the wide lace collar and cuffs.' Lucy's voice, muffled by the towel, sounded pleased. It was a very pretty dress, so simple that it stood out among other more striking dresses, and the colour, she hoped, would make her look the kind of girl a man might like to marry, elegant but demure.

She left a note for her mother on the hall table, collected an enormous cashmere shawl in which to wrap herself, and her little grey handbag, and eased her feet into her new sandals. They were a little tight, but they

were exactly right with the dress, and what was a little
discomfort compared with that?

The drawing-room looked charming with its soft
lighting and the fire blazing. She arranged herself to the
very best advantage on a small balloon-backed chair
covered in old-rose velvet, and waited for the doorbell.

The doctor was punctual to the minute, and Alice
ushered him into the drawing-room, opening the door
wide so that he had a splendid view of Lucy, delightfully
pretty and at great pains to appear cool.

She got up as he came in, and said in her best hostess
voice, 'Oh, hello again. Would you like a drink before
we go?'

'Hello, Lucy. How very elegant you look, and so
punctual. Almost unheard of and quite refreshing.'

She should have stayed in her room until he had arrived and kept him waiting, she thought crossly.

She said haughtily, 'I have to be punctual at the orphanage, it's a habit.'

'Of course. I booked a table for half-past eight; I
thought we might have a drink there first. Shall we go?'

She smiled at him, she couldn't help herself; he looked
so large and handsome and so assured. She wondered
fleetingly if he ever lost his temper.

Southampton Street wasn't all that far away, but the
evening traffic was heavy and slow moving, so it was
well past eight o'clock by the time Lucy found herself
at a table opposite the doctor. It was a good table too,
she noticed, and he was known at the restaurant. Perhaps
he took Fiona Seymour there... She wasn't going to
waste thought about that; here she was doing exactly
what she had dreamed of doing, being alone with the

doctor, nicely dressed, looking her best, and hopefully at her best when it came to conversation.

It was a pity that no witty remarks filled her head; indeed, it was regrettably empty. She sipped her sherry and thankfully bowed her head over the menu card. She was hungry and he said encouragingly, 'I dare say you had a very scanty lunch. I know I did. How about the terrine of leeks with prawns for a start, and if you like fish the red mullet is delicious—or roast pigeon?'

'I couldn't eat a pigeon,' said Lucy. 'I feed them on the way to work every morning.' She was reassured by his understanding smile. 'I'd like the red mullet.'

It wasn't until these delicacies had been eaten, followed by a dessert of puff pastry, piled with a hazelnut mousse and topped with caramel, that the doctor switched smoothly from the gentle conversation, calculated to put his companion at her ease, to the more serious subject of Miranda.

'Do you see a great deal of her at the orphanage?' he wanted to know.

'Well, yes—not all the time, of course, but always each morning, bathing her and getting her to walk and that kind of thing.'

He nodded. 'You do realise that she will probably be backward—mentally retarded—but this operation that I have just done should give her a better chance. One would wish to do everything possible for her—she is such a pretty child, and if only she had been brought to our attention while she was still a baby we could have done so much more.'

'But isn't there any special treatment? She talks a little, you know, and although she's a bit wobbly when she's walking she does try.'

'I'm going to ask you to do all you can to help her, and don't be discouraged when she makes almost no progress. I know you have a busy day and there are other children to look after, but Matron tells me that Miranda responds to you much more willingly than to anyone else there. Once the shunt gets into its stride we should take advantage of that and get her little brain stimulated. If all goes well, she will be able to have therapy in a few months.'

'Do you get many children like her?' Lucy poured their coffee and reflected sadly that the only reason he had asked her out was to make sure that she was going to stay at the orphanage and look after Miranda. Well, he need not have gone to so much trouble, wasting an evening with her when he might have been spending it with the glamorous Fiona. It was quite obvious that she had no effect upon him whatsoever, despite the fashionable grey dress and the new sandals. He probably hadn't even noticed them.

He guided their talk into more general channels, and when Lucy said that she should really go back home since she was on duty in the morning he made no objection, but signed the bill and followed her out of the restaurant without one word of persuasion to remain a little longer—or even go dancing. But that was a good thing, for the sandals were pinching horribly and walking in them, even the short distance across the pavement to the car, was crippling.

'Take them off,' suggested the doctor as he started the car.

'Oh, you don't mind? They're killing me. How did you know?'

'You have quite a fierce frown which, I hasten to add, I am quite sure no one noticed except me.' He gave her a sideways glance. 'They're quite delightful though; indeed, the rest of you looks delightful too, Lucy. Demure and malleable. Are you demure and malleable, I wonder?'

She curled her toes in blissful comfort. 'No, I don't think so; I don't think girls are demure nowadays, are they? Anyway, I'm too old...and I'm not sure what malleable means—I thought it meant squashy.'

He gave a growl of laughter. 'I meant it to mean tender and gentle, and I wasn't aware that age had anything to do with being demure. How old are you?'

'Twenty-five. You're thirty-five, aren't you?'

'We might say that we have reached the ages of discretion.'

They had reached her home and he stopped the car gently, and when she made to get out he put out a restraining hand. 'No, wait.'

He got out and opened her door. 'You'll never cram your feet back into those sandals.' He picked them up and put them into her hand, scooped her out of the seat and carried her to the front door, where he asked her to ring the doorbell.

Alice answered the door, flung it wide to allow him to get inside, and said urgently, 'You're not hurt, love? What's the matter? You've not 'ad too much to drink?'

The doctor set Lucy gently on her feet. 'Her feet,' he explained. 'Her sandals were pinching and, of course, once they were off they wouldn't go on again.'

Alice laughed. 'And there's me wondering what on earth had happened. Your mother and father are in the drawing-room—you go too, sir. I'll bring in a nice tray of coffee and you, Miss Lucy, go and fetch a pair of slippers this minute—what your ma will say I don't know.'

'It could happen to anyone,' remarked the doctor mildly, and gave Alice a nice smile so that she said,

'Oh, well, perhaps it won't be noticed,' and went ahead of them to open the drawing-room door.

Lucy's mother and father were sitting one on each side of the hearth, her father immersed in a sheaf of papers and her mother turning the pages of Harper's. They both looked up as she and the doctor went in and her father got to his feet. 'There you are, Lucy and Dr Thurloe, how delightful. Come and sit down for half an hour—Lucy, run and ask Alice to bring coffee——'

'She's making it now, Father!' Lucy bent to kiss her mother's cheek and wished she knew how to raise a graceful hand to greet the doctor in the same manner as that lady. 'Delighted to see you, Dr Thurloe. Do sit down. How very kind of you to take Lucy out to dinner.'

'It was Lucy who was kind, Mrs Lockitt,' he replied, and paused, smiling, as Mrs Lockitt caught sight of Lucy's feet.

'Lucy, your shoes? You've never lost them? You aren't hurt?'

'They pinched, Mother, so I took them off.'

'Well, really!' She turned her attention to her guest. 'I have been hoping that we might meet again, you really must dine one evening before we go to Turkey.'

'Kayseri, the ancient Hittite city—there have been some interesting finds lately, and I've been asked to go out there and take a look,' Mr Lockitt joined in. 'We plan to fly out at the end of next week.'

The doctor, much to Lucy's surprise, expressed his delight at the invitation, and Mrs Lockitt said, 'Lucy, dear, run up to my room and get my engagement book, will you? And do get some slippers at the same time.'

Lucy went slowly upstairs. Her parents, whom she loved dearly, were spoiling everything for her; she showed up in a bad light in her own home with no chance to outshine their intellectual talk—she had hardly scintillated over dinner, and since she had entered the drawing-room she had uttered only a few words. She found the book, poked her feet into a pair of frivolous satin mules and went back downstairs. Alice had brought in the coffee and Lucy's father had fetched the brandy; the doctor looked as though he had settled for the rest of the evening, already making knowledgeable replies to her father's observations—apparently he knew all about the iron-smelting activities of the Hittites, and he knew too where they had lived in Asia Minor.

As she handed round the coffee-cups he asked pleasantly, 'And do you not wish to go too, Lucy?'

Her mother answered for her. 'Lucy's a home-bird, aren't you, darling? This nice little job at the orphanage gives her something to do while we're away.' Mrs Lockitt went on, not meaning to be unkind, 'She hasn't had a training for anything. Of course, Imogen is the clever one in the family—she has this super job in the City—and Pauline works in an art gallery, and will marry at the end of this year. They are all such capable girls, and of course we have an excellent housekeeper.'

The doctor murmured politely and presently got up to go, and Mr Lockitt went to the door with him, so that beyond a stiff little speech of thanks Lucy had no chance to speak. There was nothing to say anyway. Her fragile dream, never more than a fantasy, had been blown away; he would think of her, if he ever did, as a dull girl not worth a second thought.

She bade her parents goodnight and went to bed. Surprisingly, just before she slept, she decided that somehow or other she would get to know him better, and eventually, in the teeth of all hazards, marry him.

CHAPTER THREE

FOR several days Lucy had no chance to put her resolve into practice. There was no sign of Dr Thurloe at the orphanage and it had been silly of her to imagine that she might see him there. Very occasionally in an emergency he might be asked to go there, but there weren't any emergencies; Miranda was doing very nicely—she was even showing small signs of improvement.

Mr and Mrs Lockitt, their journey arranged, had decided to invite a few friends as well as the doctor for dinner. 'Rather short notice,' observed Mrs Lockitt, 'but they're all old friends and we don't stand on ceremony. I suppose I'll have to ask Mrs Seymour...'

'Why?' asked Lucy, making a list of guests.

'Well, dear, she and Dr Thurloe seem to be old friends. Indeed, people seem to think that he might marry her— heaven knows she's trying hard enough—but I don't think he will. Mind you're home in good time and wear something pretty—the grey, perhaps?'

'Definitely not the grey. There's that rust velvet I've hardly worn...'

'Ah, yes. I'd forgotten that.' Her mother eyed her a little anxiously. 'You'll be all right while we're away, darling? It is such a pity that Pauline will be in Edinburgh at that Art Exhibition for the next two weeks, and Imogen tells me that she has to accompany Sir George to Brussels—for a few weeks, she thought. But you'll have Alice.'

'We'll be quite all right, Mother, dear. How long will you and Father be away?'

'Well, we aren't sure, it rather depends on what they've found. I must say Turkey is as good a place as anywhere to go at this time of year. Of course, we'll phone you, darling.' She smiled at Lucy. 'Now, how many have we got? I thought we might have soup first, so comforting in this weather, and then that nice fish salad and lamb chops with new potatoes and green peas—I'm sure I saw some in Harrods. They cost the earth, but they are so delicious. I'll get Alice to make some of those chocolate mousses, the ones with orange, and cheese of course.'

Lucy wrote it all down tidily and handed it to her mother.

'Thank you, dear; you're such a good daughter. I'm so glad you're not a career girl, Lucy. You must find a nice man and marry him, darling.'

Lucy said, 'Yes, Mother.' It wasn't much use telling her that she had found the nice man. The chances of marrying him, were, as far as she could see, negligible.

She dressed for the dinner party with extra care and viewed the result with some satisfaction. The rust velvet suited her—it made her eyes greener than they were, gave her hair a reflected glint, and showed off her pretty figure to its best advantage. She was even more satisfied when she joined her family in the drawing-room and her mother exclaimed, 'Why, Lucy, how delightfully that dress suits you! There's the doorbell—I've put you between Cyril and Mr Walter...'

So much for her painstaking dressing; Cyril didn't like her, she was beneath his notice, and Mr Walter was a dear, but hard of hearing. She joined in greeting the first of the guests, moving from one to the other, watching

the door out of the corner of her eye. Dr Thurloe came
in alone and she beamed at him across the room; at least
he hadn't given Fiona Seymour a lift. He smiled back
as he greeted his hostess and host, but made no effort
to join Lucy—probably because she was trapped in a
corner by old Mrs Winchell, who was eighty if she was
a day and invited to everyone's table although no one
really knew why. Lucy, listening with patience to that
lady's opinion of the government, watched Fiona
Seymour, the last to arrive, make her entrance. She really
was good-looking and this evening she was wearing a
starkly plain black dress, superbly cut, with her hair
swept into an elaborate arrangement of curls on top of
her head. She had half a dozen golden bangles on one
arm and several gold chains hung around her slender
neck. Old Mrs Winchell turned to look at her, using her
old-fashioned *lorgnettes* to do so. 'She's wasting her
time,' she muttered, and then in her usual rather loud
voice, went on to reorganise the government.

The talk at dinner was largely concerned with the
forthcoming trip to Turkey, so that Lucy was kept busy
listening first to Cyril carrying on about the rate of exchange, and then repeating to Mr Walter what people
were saying at the table that he hadn't quite heard. The
doctor, to her disappointment, was at the other end of
the rectangular table, with Imogen on one side and Fiona
on the other.

It wasn't until Mrs Winchell got up to go, forming the
spearhead of departure, that he came over to Lucy. His
casual observation that Miranda was making splendid
progress, and his equally casual hope that she wasn't
working too hard, doused any hopes she had had of

conversation of a more personal nature. She answered him woodenly and bade him a brisk goodnight.

'Goodnight, Lucy. Your eyes are very green; is that because you are bottling up bad temper? I wish I had the opportunity to find out.'

He smiled with charm and turned at the touch of Mrs Seymour's hand. She smiled too, a quite different smile from the doctor's. 'Such a nice evening, Lucy. William, will you take me home? It's only a little out of your way.'

A dismal failure, decided Lucy, reviewing her evening as she got into bed. Fiona Seymour outshone her in both looks and clothes. What was the use of just being pretty—there were hundreds of pretty girls around, but not many Fionas with their dramatic clothes and subtle make-up. Lucy sighed heavily and went to sleep to wake the next morning filled with resolve to outshine Mrs Seymour. She had no idea how to do it, but something would turn up.

Which it did, but hardly in a manner which she expected or welcomed.

Her parents left for their journey to Turkey two days later, followed first by Pauline, who flew to Edinburgh, and then, the following day, by Imogen, the picture of smart efficiency, on her way to Brussels with Sir George. They had both taken an affectionate farewell of Lucy, reiterating all the instructions she had had from her mother and leaving their telephone numbers prominently displayed. The house seemed empty after they had gone, even though Alice and the daily cleaner had seized the opportunity to clean the place from attic to cellar. Lucy was glad to go to bed early and got up betimes in the morning, remembering in delight that today she would take Miranda to the City Royal to have a check-up by Dr Thurloe. It would be all very professional, of course, but at least Fiona Seymour wouldn't be there. The clinic was in the early afternoon; the morning seemed endless, and she had a few bad moments when Matron couldn't make up her mind if Lucy should go with Miranda or stay and take care of the smallest orphans whose usual attendant had gone off sick.

Lucy, her face serene, her insides churning, waited for Matron to decide and heaved a sigh of relief when that lady's eye fell on Miranda working herself into a rage with the girl who was to take Lucy's place.

'Oh, well—you'd better take her; they'll want her as quiet as possible at the clinic and she's getting quite worked up. I'll take over the little ones while you're gone. Perhaps you won't be away too long.'

So Lucy and Miranda set off together in the ambu-lance which had been sent for them and arrived to find the waiting-room packed to the doors. Outpatients Sister saw her come in and hurried towards her. 'There's been a delay,' she explained. 'Dr Thurloe was called away ur-gently just as we were starting. Luckily you're in the first ten to be seen so it shouldn't be too long. He'll be here any minute now.'

She bustled away and Lucy sat down, Miranda on her lap, grizzling a little because she didn't much like her surroundings. Lucy wasn't too keen either; it was a chilly blustery day, but the waiting-room was warm and stuffy—moreover, the babies and toddlers were noisy. That was only to be expected, of course, but after a time it was wearing to the nerves.

It was an hour before it was Miranda's turn and by then she was cross and whining fretfully despite Lucy's efforts to keep her amused. Lucy carried the child into the consulting-room, sat her down on the couch and wished the doctor a good afternoon. He said in a detached manner, 'Ah, yes—Miranda. I'll need to look at that shunt.' He looked tired and she wasn't surprised—having to deal with dozens of babies and children, all ill, all in various stages of peevishness, he must be exhausted. He smiled down at her suddenly. 'Hello, Lucy,' and then, 'You look hot and a bit cross...'

'I'm not cross, but I am hot. Half London's sitting out there.'

He nodded. 'If you'll get Miranda's things off I'll take a look.'

It was at that moment that there was a loud bang and all the lights went out. And moments later a voice screamed, 'It's a bomb!'

Lucy, her arms around Miranda, stayed where she was. The doctor's voice, swearing richly, sounded reassuring, and a moment later he had turned on a torch from his desk. 'Don't move,' he commanded. That was something she wouldn't have dreamed of doing anyway. 'The auxiliary lighting will come on in a moment. I'm going into the waiting-room...'

The din was fearful, children screaming and frantic mothers calling and, from the sound of it, everyone rushing to and fro. She could hear the doctor's voice, raised in a commanding bellow, urging everyone to stay where they were, but panic had taken over, for the lights hadn't gone on again and those people nearest the doors had rushed to open them, but, because of the press people behind them, had been unable to do so. The clinic was situated in the semi-basement of the hospital and depended entirely upon artificial light, and the dark was

Stygian. The door to the waiting-room burst wide open
suddenly, and in no time at all the consulting-room was
crammed with people all talking at once while the
children screamed and the babies cried. Lucy got a good
grip of Miranda and took a deep breath.

'Be quiet and stand still!' she shouted urgently, and,
although her lung power was nothing like as powerful
as the doctor's, some of the women around her heard
and there was a moment's lull broken only by infant
wailing. 'Keep still,' she urged, 'you're safe enough as
long as you don't rush around. Do think of the children.
The doors will be opened as soon as possible and there's
auxiliary lighting.'

There was a good deal of murmuring and shuffling,
but at least the frantic pushing and shoving seemed to
have stopped. She could hear the noise in the waiting-
room and see the flash of torches here and there; she
heard the outpatients sister's calm voice and then the
doctor, his voice loud and calm, as he made his way
towards the doors.

She didn't understand why there was such a long delay
before the doors were at last opened and at the same
time the lights came on again. And then she knew the
reason. They had been blocked by the first to reach them
who, unable to get the doors open, had been pushed or
knocked down by those behind them, frantic to get out
too.

The waiting-room was in a state of chaos. Sister and
the two nurses who were with her were already shep-
herding some of the mothers and children towards the
further end of the waiting-room and out through the
door there, while the doctor, head and shoulders above
everyone else, waded to and fro through the mass of

people, carrying children and babies away from the doors. Sister came back and poked her head round the consulting-room door. 'Everyone all right here? Come with me to the casualty-room and we'll check all of you and the children.'

There were a great many people in the waiting-room now, moving the injured away, comforting frightened children and still shaken mothers. Lucy picked up Miranda and followed the trickle of women leaving the clinic. There was no reason to stay—obviously the doctor had his hands full with his helpers, handing back babies and children to their mothers, and checking that no one was seriously hurt. In Casualty a nurse was taking names, making sure that no one was hurt or badly shocked, and cups of tea were being offered. To Casualty Sister's enquiry as to whether she felt able to get back on her own she answered calmly that she felt fine, but it would be best if she got Miranda back to her familiar surroundings as quickly as possible.

'You look a sensible girl,' said Sister. 'As soon as we can, we'll let Matron at the Orphanage know when you can come back.' She glanced at a restless Miranda. 'Dr Thurloe did a shunt, didn't he? I expect he'll want to see her just as soon as we've cleared up the mess in his clinic.'

There were a great many women sitting about, drinking their tea and mulling over the excitement of the afternoon; quite a few were to be taken home by ambulance, declaring that they were shaken too badly to get on a bus. Lucy made her way to Casualty entrance and into the street. It had begun to rain, a gentle drizzle which seeped through her clothes as she waited for a taxi. Miranda was well wrapped up, but she hated the rain and began to wail; it was a relief when a taxi stopped and Lucy got thankfully inside. Miranda was heavy, and she had to be held carefully.

By the time they reached the orphanage, the toddler was crying in earnest. Lucy paid off the cabby and hurried inside, to get Miranda's clothes off as quickly as possible and ask one of the girls to tell Matron that they were back.

That excellent woman took in the situation at a glance; she sent someone for a cup of tea for Lucy, milk and biscuits for Miranda and then got her into her cot, all the while listening to Lucy's succinct account of the mishap at the clinic.

'It would have been all right if someone hadn't shouted that it was a bomb,' she remarked, 'but of course it was very dark, and once everyone started rushing around it was impossible to stop them, although Dr Thurloe was roaring like a bull. He had a torch, and so, after a few minutes, did Sister, but the clinic is a big place and it was packed with people.'

'And where were you?'

'In the consulting-room. Dr Thurloe was just about to examine Miranda. Sister said she'd let you know when we could go back to the clinic. It was hopeless to go on this afternoon, I think there were several people hurt when they got knocked over by the doors.'

'A mercy it was no worse. You're wet, aren't you. Get that coat off and drink your tea. When you've fed Miranda, go home, Lucy; it's already almost five and you'll be here as usual in the morning?'

'Of course, Matron. I'm sorry that Miranda has to go again, she does so hate it there. I think the noise bothers her.'

'Poor scrap. But we can't ask someone as important as Dr Thurloe to visit here unless it is an emergency or something serious. I might ask one of his registrars to come and see her here.'

It was six o'clock by the time Lucy got home; Miranda hadn't wanted her tea and it had taken time and patience to coax her to eat it, and when Lucy had at last left the orphanage it was to find the bus queue stretching for yards along the pavement. When she finally got home Alice came into the hall at the sound of her key in the lock.

'I was getting worried!' she exclaimed. 'You not home at your usual time—what 'appened?' She bustled Lucy out of her coat. 'All wet you are, and looking as though you could do with a nice cuppa.'

'Oh, Alice, I could. Look, I'll have a shower and change and then come down to the kitchen and tell you all about it.'

'Righto, love. And put on something warm, you look fair chilled.'

Fifteen minutes later Lucy went back downstairs. She had left her hair loose and had got into a thick green sweater and a tweed skirt and she felt a good deal better; a pot of tea would be heaven. She hoped that Alice had been inspired to make a plate of toast too. She opened the kitchen door and danced in. 'Alice...'

Alice was standing there all right, but so was Dr Thurloe, standing at the window, watching the feet of passers-by. He turned round as she came to a surprised standstill. 'Forgive me for calling at this unreasonable hour, but I wanted to make sure that you were all right after this afternoon's incident. I've seen Miranda, she's

none the worse luckily. But you? You were all right?
You stayed where you were?'

She nodded, trying to think of something to say and
failing.

'Good. It could have been much worse, but several
women were injured in the rush to get away and I've
had to admit four children.' He frowned and she saw
that he was concerned as well as angry.

'Well, you did all you could,' she said. 'I could hear
you telling everyone to stay in their seats. It must have
been impossible to move out there.'

'Yes. Panic is a terrifying thing. I'll make sure that it
never happens again. It just so happened that the auxiliary lighting was being checked when the electricity
failed—some workman accidentally severed a cable.'

'Oh, was that the bang?' She had a strong wish to put
her arms around him and tell him that it wasn't his fault,
although she knew that he felt responsible. 'Alice has
made a pot of tea; would you like to have a cup?'

She didn't wait for him to answer, but fetched the
teapot and put it on the tray Alice had set on the table,
collected another cup and saucer from the dresser and
sat down at the table while Alice fetched the plate of
buttered toast from the Aga.

'Now just you sit there and enjoy your tea,' she advised them, 'while I pop up to your ma and pa's room
and get it straight now it's been cleaned.'

She took herself off, looking pleased because the
doctor had held the kitchen door open for her. He closed
it and came and sat down opposite Lucy.

'I'm sorry you had to find your own way back,' he
told her. 'Sister told me that you were going to get a
taxi. Did you have to wait?'

'Only for a few minutes.' She passed the toast. 'Do you like strawberry jam? Alice made a batch last summer...' She got up and fetched a pot from a cupboard, found a spoon and handed it across the table.

They sat munching their toast thickly layered with jam, and since there was nothing more to be said about the afternoon's happening their talk became rather more personal. At least, the questions the doctor put were gently probing—so gentle, in fact, that Lucy didn't realise how much she was telling him. For her part she would have dearly loved to have asked him any number of questions, but she wasn't quite sure how to begin. He wasn't married, that she did know, but what about Mrs Seymour? And did he have any family? A mother, a father, brothers and sisters? She wished very much that she had either of her sisters' self-assurance; she was sure that neither of them would have hesitated.

The doctor's quiet voice broke into her thoughts. 'How long will your mother and father be away?' he wanted to know.

'It depends—if it's something interesting I expect they'll be in Turkey for some time.'

'You are not lonely? Your mother told me that your sisters would be away too.'

'Only for a week or two and I've got Alice, and Mrs Simpkins.'

His raised eyebrows looked a question. 'Our cat. She's in the airing cupboard with her kittens. I suppose you wouldn't like a kitten? Not yet, of course, they're only a few weeks old.'

'Er—my housekeeper has an elderly cat, a matron christened, through some misunderstanding—Thomas— I dare say she might like to have a kitten to mother.'

Here was a crumb of information, better than nothing.
'Have you a dog?'

'Two—Robinson and Friday; they like cats.'

Lucy laughed. 'Did you rescue them off a desert
island?'

'In a manner of speaking.'

She poured more tea for them both. 'What breed are
they?'

'A little bit of everything, I should imagine. You like
dogs?'

She nodded. 'Only we can't have one; Father and
Mother are away so much, Imogen and Pauline wouldn't
have the time and I'm away all day too.'

'You don't need to work,' he suggested gently.

'Oh, no, but you see I had to do something; I can't
just be at home. I—I found this job, I wanted to do
something useful; I'm not clever, you see, and it's difficult to have a career unless you're clever.'

'Would you not rather prefer to marry?' He spoke
with a casual kindness which prompted her to reply.

'Oh, yes, only no one's asked me.'

'You surprise me, you must know that you're a pretty
girl.'

It didn't enter her head to be coy about it. 'Yes, but
I'm hopelessly shy and I don't know how to talk to
people,' and at his quizzical look, 'I can talk to you.'

He agreed gravely, although there was a gleam of
amusement in his eyes. 'I have enjoyed our talk and my
tea.' He glanced at his watch. 'I am only sorry that I
have to go out this evening.' He watched Lucy's face
assume a wooden politeness. Her eyes, he noted with
interest, were quite blindingly green.

'Of course. It was kind of you to call. I hope no one was badly hurt this afternoon.'

'Fortunately not. I should like to get my hands on whoever it was who screamed that it was a bomb.' He smiled at her. 'Thank you for my tea, Lucy.'

She went to the door with him and ushered him out, and then closed and locked the door behind him. Well, she knew a little more about him now, but she doubted very much if she would learn much more; she wasn't likely to see anything of him other than at the clinic, and probably Miranda wouldn't need to go again for a long time. Still, there was today's visit to be repeated, although he wouldn't have anything to say to her other than instructions to convey to Matron.

She cleared away the tea things and Alice came back into the kitchen, 'Gorn, 'as 'e?' Mostly she was careful with her aitches, but if she was disturbed or excited she tended to overlook them. 'I could 'ave cooked him a bite of supper.'

'He's going out,' Lucy was putting away the jam, 'he told me so.'

'That Mrs Seymour—the cook at number eleven knows 'er maid, says she's after 'im, ringing 'im up at all hours and cross as two sticks when 'e's not there or got something better to do. The cook told me that this maid says 'e's wedded to his work.'

Which cheered Lucy up. One could always marry a man who was wedded to his work, but not one who was wedded to Mrs Seymour. But all she said was, 'Well, he's old enough to make up his own mind, I expect, don't you, Alice?' She said it in a bright voice and Alice took a look at her.

'Men,' said Alice, and clashed a saucepan. Lucy had always been her favourite and she had seen the look on her face.

Lucy took Miranda to the clinic two days later, and although Dr Thurloe was there there was no chance to speak to him other than to say good afternoon and goodbye. This time there was a staff nurse there who whisked Miranda away for X-ray and tests and Lucy was politely asked to wait in the waiting-room. Miranda bawled to high heaven and on their return from X-ray and Path Lab the staff nurse handed her over to Lucy with a sigh of relief. 'My goodness, she's a handful,' she observed. 'Dr Thurloe wants her back in the consulting-room for a minute or two. Will you take her?'

Miranda, scarlet with rage still, sniffed and snuffled into Lucy's shoulder, but she had stopped screaming and allowed the doctor to examine her head; she even, after a few doubtful glances, smiled at him. He smiled back. Lucy was the only one with an expressionless face, all at sea as to how to behave. One minute the man was eating toast and jam in her mother's kitchen and the next sitting there as remote and grave as a judge. She played safe and said nothing at all.

He finished at length and by then the staff nurse was back again.

'I'll write to her doctor and let your matron have a copy. Miranda's progress is very satisfactory—I'll see her again in a month.' His smile was pleasant and detached. 'Goodbye, Lucy.'

She bade him goodbye gravely, then took Miranda back to the orphanage and got on with the rest of her day's chores. She was disappointed, but she wasn't downcast; she wasn't sure how to beat Fiona Seymour at her own game, but she was certain that she would get a chance to try. She was quite sure that she would make the doctor a splendid wife, just as she was equally certain that Mrs Seymour would ruin his life for him. When she got home she got out the telephone directory and found his name and address—a house by the river in Chiswick, one of a row of charming old houses with a frontage on the Thames and as peaceful a spot as one could wish for in London. She put the directory away thoughtfully; he had two dogs who would have to be exercised. Richmond Park or Kew Gardens seemed the obvious places for their run; he could take the car easily enough to either—probably not every day, she decided, as there must be quiet streets near his home where he could walk them, but at the weekends...

Her sisters were still away, and Alice saw nothing strange in her announcement that she intended having a nice long walk on the following Sunday. 'And I'll not be back for lunch, Alice,' said Lucy. 'If it's a nice day I could do with some fresh air.'

'I'll cut you a sandwich or two,' said Alice. 'Where are you going?'

'Richmond Park or Kew, I haven't quite decided.'

'Well, be careful, love, don't go off down any lonely paths. I'm not sure that your ma...'

'I'll stay on the main walks, Alice, and I'll be back for tea. Do you want to go to church?'

'In the evening—I'll have something in the Aga for supper.'

Lucy considered it a good omen that Sunday morning should be all sunshine and blue sky even though it was cooled by a March wind. She wore a new mohair sweater in shades of green to match her eyes, and a pleated tweed skirt; she tucked a scarf into her shoulder-bag, and, after a splendid breakfast and five minutes' listening to Alice's warnings, caught a bus. The temptation to take a look at the doctor's house was great, but she prudently skirted it and started to walk in the direction of Richmond Park. It had been silly of her to get off the bus on an impulse; now she got on the bus once more and stayed on it until it reached the park. She had had to chose between Richmond Park and Kew Gardens, she couldn't be in both at once, and really, she reflected as she began to walk along one of the main paths, she was being childish in the extreme. She had had no idea that falling in love with someone entailed so much planning and plotting which was more than likely to no avail.

There were quite a few people about, most of them with dogs and children, and presently she began to enjoy herself. It was lovely to get away from the streets and houses, and as she walked she allowed herself to day-dream: a cottage in the country, just for weekends, where the children could play while she and William gardened and Robinson and Friday roamed at will. A large garden, she decided, full of old-fashioned flowers and roses and with a large lawn where they could all play croquet. She wandered off the path a little way and sat down on a fallen log. Four children, she decided, two of each; the boys would be doctors like their father, and the girls would be pretty and clever besides. And she and William would grow old gracefully together—he would make a handsome old man... She looked up and saw him coming towards her, still fortunately on the right side of forty and certainly handsome.

He had the dogs with him; a small, nondescript dog with a curly black coat and a whiskered face who pranced up to her and offered his head for a scratch, and a shaggy-coated dog with a mild face and a splendid tail. He was very large and lumbered up to Lucy and bent over her, breathing gently on her face, and she pulled at his ear, glad of something to do for the doctor was standing in front of her, looking down at her heightened colour with amused interest.

'You're a long way from home,' he said, and he sat down beside her.

Lucy tickled the little dog under his chin and didn't look at him. 'It is a lovely day, and it's nice to get away from the streets and just walk.'

He nodded gravely. 'I come here every Sunday when I'm free, and quite often after breakfast for half an hour, once the mornings get light. Until then we have to make do with a brisk walk round the houses.'

'They're nice dogs,' said Lucy, 'and quite different.' She ventured a look at her companion. 'Did you get them from Battersea Dogs' Home?'

'No—Robinson,' he patted the large dog on a massive shoulder, 'was thrown out of a car on a motorway, and I happened to be behind the car, and Friday was left in a cardboard box on the side of the road.'

'How utterly beastly,' said Lucy fiercely, 'to do a thing like that to an animal! I'm so glad you were there—they must love you . . .'

'They're great company and they make a nice change from babies and children.'

Lucy turned an alarmed face to his. 'Oh, don't you like babies and children?'

'Of course I do—I wouldn't be a paediatrician otherwise, would I?'

'Oh, sorry, that was a silly thing to say.'

They sat in silence for a minute or so while she searched wildly for something to talk about; if he didn't speak soon she would have to get up and go. He stayed silent and she sighed soundlessly with her disappointment and said cheerfully, 'Well, I must be on my way. It was nice meeting Robinson and Friday.' She started to get up and put on her scarf, and he put out a large gentle hand and pulled her down again.

'Do you have to be home for lunch? Or are you meeting someone?' he asked.

She shook her head.

'Good, then let us walk together for a while. I've got the car here, I'll drive you back when you want to go.' He glanced at his watch. 'It's still early—if we take the next path on the left there's a coffee kiosk there.'

She didn't have to worry about something to talk about, for the doctor embarked on a meandering conversation which needed few or no replies. By the time they had reached the kiosk she felt quite at ease, so much so that she only just stopped herself in time from telling him that she had come to the park in the hope of meeting him. She went bright red at the thought and the doctor eyed her thoughtfully, wondering why she looked quite guilty—it could be nothing he had said, he was sure of that; maybe something she had thought . . .?

He said easily, 'You'll have coffee? Why not sit down on that bench and I'll fetch it?'

He wandered off, and the dogs, having drunk noisily from the bowl of water by the kiosk, followed him. They all came back very shortly, and, while the dogs roamed round close by, they drank their coffee. It was strong and hot and Lucy remembered the sandwiches Alice had packed for her. She offered them shyly and the doctor took one. 'Your Alice must be a treasure. My house-keeper runs her pretty close, she's a marvellous cook too. Which reminds me that I have to be back for lunch. Sunday is the one day when I can have people in.'

The bright morning lost its brightness; Lucy brushed crumbs from her gentle mouth and stood up at once. 'I don't suppose you have a great deal of time to meet your friends,' she remarked politely. 'Do you go to the hospital every day?'

'No, twice a week for rounds and outpatients, and one theatre day; I have a private practice too, and I'm consultant to a couple of other hospitals.'

'My goodness, don't you ever get tired?'

'Oh, yes.' They were walking back to the main path once more, and presently they were at the gates and a few minutes later in the Rolls with the dogs sitting primly side by side in the back.

The journey back was far too short, but not so short that Lucy didn't have the leisure to reflect upon the abject failure of her plan. She had been most successful in meeting him, true enough, but it had got her nowhere.

CHAPTER FOUR

DR THURLOE got out when they reached Lucy's home, went with her to the door and waited until she had gone inside, declining her invitation to come in for a drink, as she had known he would. She hadn't wanted to ask him, but the social niceties had to be observed. She remarked suitably on the pleasures of her morning walk with him and bade him a cheerful goodbye. In the hall, with the closed door between them, she allowed herself a long sigh. All the same she had got to know him just a little more. The dogs, his housekeeper, guests for Sunday lunch—Fiona, of course. Lucy ground her perfect teeth at the thought.

'Back already?' asked Alice, putting her head round the kitchen door. She added innocently, 'Thought I heard a car.'

'You did. I met Dr Thurloe walking his dogs and he drove me back.'

'Didn't he want to come in for coffee?' asked Alice sharply.

'Well, no. We had some in Richmond Park, he's got guests for lunch.'

Alice made a tutting sound. 'A day in the fresh air would do 'im more good, and 'im stuck in that 'ospital all day and every day.'

'He doesn't go every day, he goes to other hospitals too, and he's got a private practice.'

'That's as may be, 'e still 'as to treat patients, doesn't 'e? From morn till night, and know what 'e's talking about too, and stuck in a stuffy room with germs being breathed all over 'im.'

She sounded indignant and Lucy made haste to agree; put like that the doctor merited sympathy, although he hadn't looked as though he needed it that morning.

'He needs a good wife,' declared Alice, and Lucy agreed in a suitably casual voice.

Pauline came back from Edinburgh the following week and was instantly plunged into a new exhibition at the art gallery. 'There's a preview on Saturday,' she told Lucy, and, 'You're coming, I've got a ticket for you.'

'I'm working on Saturday morning...'

'I know that, darling—the exhibition is in the afternoon. Three o'clock, you'll have plenty time to dress up and get a taxi. I'll be on the look-out for you. Have you bought any new clothes yet?'

'No. I've not had any time.'

'It'll be a dressy affair. Wear that brown velvet suit and the Liberty scarf I gave you for Christmas.'

'All right. What kind of pictures are they?'

'Abstract.'

'Lines and squiggles? I can't make head or tail of them.'

'You don't have to, Lucy—just look interested.' Pauline added fretfully, 'I thought you'd enjoy it.'

'Oh, but I shall,' said Lucy quickly, 'and it's sweet of you to ask me.'

And indeed it was nice to have something to look forward to. The orphans took up most of her days, but there was still too much time in which to brood over Dr Thurloe. An outing might take him off her mind for a time at least. There had been no sign of him, but then why should there be? Miranda was settling down nicely and her next appointment wasn't for more than two weeks, and since Lucy's parents were away there was no chance of meeting him at a dinner party or drinks, for no one had thought of inviting her without them.

Her mother telephoned when she could, but, as she pointed out, they were sometimes in remote regions and it wasn't always possible. Her father was full of enthusiasm, she had told Lucy; excavations had uncovered evidence of a high level of civilisation more than a thousand years B.C. There was no question of their coming home for several weeks at least. Each time she asked, 'You're well, darling?' and without waiting for an answer said, 'That's good. Have a lovely time—I'll ring again when I can.'

A letter would have been more satisfactory, but Lucy doubted if her mother would have much chance to sit down and write letters, and she had been told not to write to them since they were moving around so much.

Lucy had plenty of time to dress on Saturday. The exhibition opened at three o'clock, and if she took a taxi she didn't need to leave home until ten minutes or so before the hour; she didn't want to be the first to arrive. Pauline wasn't coming home for lunch—she would have it with Cyril, who would, of course, be at the exhibition too. Lucy got into the brown suit and draped the lovely scarf around her shoulders and, after due thought, got into her high-heeled brown kid shoes. She wasn't keen on very high heels, but they looked good with the suit.

There were a great many people already at the art gallery when she got there. She took the proffered brochure and edged her way through the first room looking for Pauline. It was Cyril whom she first met.

He greeted her pompously. 'Pauline is besieged by eager viewers,' he told her. 'As soon as she is free she will come to you. I would offer my services in accompanying you round the room, but I feel that I should be at Pauline's side.'

'Oh, of course you must,' said Lucy, and wondered how her sister could bear him—and for the rest of her life, too. 'I'll start in this room and work my way round. Do let Pauline know and tell her not to worry about me.'

Cyril allowed himself to be swept away by a surge of people and she was left to examine the exhibits.

She went slowly from one to the other, glad that she had the brochure, for otherwise she wouldn't have had the least idea what they were. She had reached the end of one wall and was starting on the next, contemplating a large square upon which were a series of lines and a few dots, when Dr Thurloe's voice, low in her ear, murmured, 'Noughts and crosses? Enlighten me, Lucy.'

She chuckled. 'It's called *Maiden with a Bucket . . .*'

'You astound me, any one of your orphans could do better.'

'Why are you—that is, do you like modern art?'

'No.' He sounded quite certain about it. 'Your sister very kindly sent me a ticket and it seemed churlish not to come. Do people actually buy these—these scribbles?'

'Oh, yes. Pauline works here, you know; she says it's a most successful and lucrative aspect of the art world.'

'Do you like them?' He looked down at her and thought how pretty she looked in that brown thing and how ridiculous her high heels were.

'Me? No. I have tried to because of Pauline, but I do agree with you that the orphans are better at it. There's Pauline...'

He took her arm and edged through the crowd and Pauline saw them and came towards them. 'There you are—and Dr Thurloe. How nice! This is so successful. Lucy, I won't be home until late, you'll be all right? I'll go back with Cyril to his flat and have dinner with him.'

She smiled widely at them and turned away with a quick 'bye' as an Arab in flowing robes accosted her.

Lucy had gone very pink. It was tiresome that Pauline had said all that about coming home late and would she be all right with the doctor standing there. Now he might possibly feel that the least he could do was to see her back home. She said hurriedly, 'Well, I'll say goodbye. I came to please Pauline, and I must fly or I'll be late.' She offered a hand. 'It was nice meeting you again.'

He took her hand, but he didn't let it go. They stood, rather close together because of the squash of people around them, and looked at each other while Lucy's pink face went slowly red and the doctor's firm mouth widened into a smile.

He said quietly, 'Could we escape together, do you think? And will you believe me when I say that I intended asking you to come to tea with me as soon as I saw you here?'

'I'd love a cup of tea,' said Lucy, quite sure that he would never lie to her or anyone else unless it was absolutely necessary.

He took her arm again and they went out of the gallery into the quiet Saturday afternoon street. 'The car's just round the corner.'

When they were in the car she asked, 'Where are we going?'

'My home—Mrs Trump likes the idea of having a kitten, but you ought to have a word with her first, don't you think?'

Which sounded reasonable enough.

She gave a small sigh of pleasure as she got out of the car in front of his house. It was the end one of the row of old houses in Strand on the Green, facing the river, pristine in its black and white paintwork and shining brass door knocker. There was a tub filled with snow-drops at each side of the door, and staring at them from the window alongside the door was a very large, fat tabby cat.

'Thomas,' said Lucy happily, and when the doctor opened his door she went past him into the narrow, high-ceilinged hall. It smelled of beeswax polish and very faintly of lavender, and the console-table and the two chairs on either side of it gleamed with years of loving care. There was a fine silk rug on the floor, and the walls were panelled waist-high, and above that the paper was a soft dim crimson.

The doctor caught her by the arm and swept her through a half-open door into a room with windows facing the water, and the cat got down off the window-seat and came to meet them, taking no notice of the sudden rush and barking of Robinson and Friday. She offered an elderly head for a rub and then, with her tail high and ignoring the dogs, went out of the room, to return almost at once, walking sedately beside Mrs Trump, a short, stout lady with a round happy face, a great deal of grey hair held up by combs and skewered ruthlessly by hairpins, and faded blue eyes.

'There you are, sir. And you'd like a nice cup of tea, I've no doubt.' She beamed at Lucy. 'And the young lady too. Trump will have the tea-tray in five minutes. Would the young lady like to refresh herself?'

Lucy was conscious of the doctor's amused glance. She darted a smile at him and said sedately, 'If I might leave my jacket somewhere?'

'This is Miss Lockitt, Mrs Trump; will you see that she has all she wants?'

'Indeed, I will, sir. You come with me, miss, if you would be so kind.'

Lucy followed her into the hall and then into a cloakroom under the gracefully curving staircase at the back of the hall. As she took off her jacket and set the very pale pink blouse to rights, she reflected that her mother wasn't the only one who could boast about her faithful housekeeper—obviously Mrs Trump was a treasure, and presumably the Trump she had mentioned would be her husband and another treasure.

The cloakroom, though small, contained everything needed for the maintainance of cleanliness and beauty. She left it, as Mrs Trump had put it, feeling refreshed and ready to make the most of an hour's company with the doctor.

He got up as she went back into the drawing-room, and the dogs got up with him and fussed around while he settled her in a chair by the fire. She looked around the room, warm, charmingly furnished and softly lit, and then at him sitting opposite her. Dear, darling William, she reflected dreamily, she was getting to know him after all; the gods, or whoever arranged these things, were on her side.

She couldn't stop her delighted smile, and he said kindly, 'You like my home, Lucy?'

'Oh, my goodness, it's perfect—what I've seen of it. It's not like living in London here, is it?'

The door opened before he could answer and a middle-aged, rotund man carrying a tray came in. He bade the doctor a grave good afternoon and repeated his greeting to Lucy when he was introduced. 'Mr and Mrs Trump have been with me for more years than I care to remember. My life would fall apart without them, wouldn't it, Trump?'

'There is that possibility, sir; I trust the occasion may never arise.' He lifted the lid of a silver muffin dish. 'Mrs Trump thought that a muffin might be acceptable, sir—such a chilly afternoon.'

'Muffins will be specially good, Trump. Switch the phone through to this room, will you? And have your own tea in peace.'

'Thank you, sir.' Trump made his stately way out of the room and Lucy was begged to pour the tea.

An hour passed pleasantly. Lucy, comfortably full of muffins and Madeira cake, had lost all count of time; she was far too busy probing delicately for details of the doctor's way of life, an exercise which was affording him a good deal of secret amusement. It was in a brief pause in their conversation that the long case clock by the door chimed a musical six o'clock, and she jumped to her feet like a guilty child. 'Oh, the time—I'm so sorry, I do hope I haven't delayed you. I dare say you're doing something if you're free...'

He didn't deny it. 'Plenty of time and only a few friends coming to dinner. I'll run you home.' He smiled at her very kindly. 'I have enjoyed our afternoon, we must do it again some time.'

Lucy smiled and murmured and her green eyes belied the smile. Nothing, she vowed silently, nothing would induce her to accept any invitation from him again. It was so obvious to her now that he had taken pity on her and sat, probably bored stiff, for two hours listening to her uninspired remarks. She paused in the doorway to say, 'There's really no need to drive me back, there'll be a bus at the end of the street...'

A waste of breath, for he said nothing at all, but summoned Mrs Trump with Lucy's jacket, helped her into it and ushered her out of his front door and into the Rolls-Royce parked there. She was far too cross to listen to his easy flow of talk as he drove her back to Chelsea, and almost before he had stopped in front of her house she had started to open her door.

A large hand came down on hers. 'Stay where you are,' he advised her, and got out of the car to open her door and help her out. He took her key from her and opened the house door, at the same time giving the door knocker a thump so that Alice came from the kitchen.

'There you are,' said Alice. 'I was just wondering where you'd got to.' She beamed at the doctor. 'You'll come in, sir?'

'Thank you, no, Alice.' He glanced at Lucy, standing silent and still cross, feeling like a child brought home from a party and handed over to Nanny.

'Thank you for my tea,' she said frostily. 'Goodbye, Dr Thurloe.'

'Goodbye Lucy. Shall you be in Richmond Park tomorrow morning?'

'No, I'm going out with a friend.'

She slipped past Alice and she heard him wish the housekeeper goodnight before he got back into his car and drove away.

Alice shut the door. 'Had a nice time, did you, Miss Lucy?'

Lucy heaved a great sigh. 'No, I did not, it was absolutely beastly.' She burst into tears and raced up to her room, and didn't come down until Alice came to tell her that her supper was ready in the dining-room.

'What time will you be going out tomorrow, Miss Lucy?' Alice wanted to know. 'To see these friends of yours?'

'I only said that,' explained Lucy, 'because I was afraid the doctor might take pity on me again...'

'Take pity on you? Whatever do you mean, love? He's the last man to waste 'is time, or I'm a Dutchman. If he wanted to take you out 'e'd 'ave meant it.'

Lucy shook her head. 'Oh, no, Alice dear, he's a kind man, and Pauline asked me if I'd be all right on my own with you, and he was there and he asked me to have tea with him at his house.' She added a little wildly, 'Just as he'd give a stray dog a good meal or feed a lost kitten...' She paused. 'Oh, dear, and that's why I went, because he said his housekeeper would like one of Mrs Simpkins' kittens and I was supposed to talk to her about it.'

'Never mind,' said Alice comfortably. 'You'll be bound to see him again.'

'Not if I can help it,' said Lucy, so fiercely that Alice gave her a sharp look. 'You go and sit by the sitting-room fire,' was all she said, 'and I'll bring you your coffee.'

'I'll help you wash up...'

'That you will not, I've had all day to idle away, and all the other days as well now there's no one here but you. Miss Pauline'll be back tonight?'

'She's going to Cyril's place for dinner, and I think she intends to spend the weekend with his parents and come back tomorrow evening. I'm sure Imogen will be back in a few days—I had a letter.'

When Alice brought the coffee she made the good soul sit down. 'You just stay there,' she ordered nicely and fetched a cup and saucer from the dining-room sideboard. 'Look, Alice, I don't want to do anything tomorrow, only wash my hair and do my nails and loll around with the Sunday papers. Wouldn't you like to take the day off—which you can while you have the chance? You'll be busy enough when Imogen and Pauline and my parents are back.'

'Your lunch——?' began Alice.

'I can cook, you know I can, you taught me. There's food in the fridge?'

'Of course there is,' Alice declared indignantly, 'but it's my place to cook...'

'Oh, Alice, of course it is, you shall cook me a luscious supper when you get back. You know you're dying to see your sister. Go after breakfast and come back after tea. I know Mother would approve.'

'You'll be all right alone? I'm not sure...'

'Oh, go on, Alice,' wheedled Lucy. 'I'm twenty-five, you know, and able to look after myself.'

'Oh, well, it would be nice to go over to Golders Green for an hour or two. But you're to phone me if I'm needed.'

'I promise, Alice.'

The house was quiet once Alice had gone the next morning. Lucy roamed around, played with the kittens, washed her hair and did her nails and then curled up with the Sunday papers. But she didn't read them for long; she went over Saturday's events, almost word for word. 'The trouble is,' she told Mrs Simpkins, who was sitting in her basket with her kittens, 'that I behaved like a silly girl. I'm a grown woman of twenty-five, and that's getting on, but I simply have no idea how to sparkle, though I dare say William wouldn't want that kind of a wife. It's nice to take out someone that looks like that odious Fiona, all gush and black velvet, but she'd be no good at all at the breakfast table if he'd been up half the night slaving over some ill child. I'd do very nicely, you know.'

She wandered into the kitchen and switched on the coffee percolator and found the biscuit tin. The front door bell jangled and she frowned. It could be Pauline and Cyril, or Imogen returned several days early. It could be anyone. She went to the door and opened it, remembering just too late to put up the chain first; it could be a thief.

It was Dr Thurloe and she gaped at him, colour flooding her face. She said idiotically, 'Oh, it's you.'

'Indeed it is I. On my way back for lunch from the park I thought I'd give your housekeeper a message for you about the kitten.' He smiled slowly. 'You changed your mind about spending the day with your friends?'

She said breathlessly, 'Well, yes—no, actually I wasn't going anywhere.'

He said smoothly, 'In that case will you come back with me for lunch? There will be one or two friends— quite informal. Come as you are.'

She gave silent thanks that she had put on a rather nice jersey dress that morning. She said uncertainly, 'Yes, but you weren't expecting me...'

'Another one more or less won't upset Mrs Trump, and I should be delighted if you could come.'

Her resolve not to accept any invitations from him dissolved like jelly in hot water. 'Well, thank you, I'd like to come.'

'In that case may I come in and collect a kitten?'

'Oh, yes, of course, they're in the kitchen. Do you know which one Mrs Trump would like to have?'

'Thomas is a Tabby, so perhaps a contrast? Black and white or ginger.'

She led the way to the kitchen where Mrs Simpkins, bored with her kittens, was stretched out before the Aga. The kittens were charming. They were looked at in turn, and finally the doctor chose the ugliest, if a kitten could ever be called ugly, but she had a large nose and a flat head and very round eyes. Mrs Simpkins merely yawned when Lucy took her to say goodbye, and took no notice when the doctor tucked her under one arm.

'Would you like a cup of coffee?' asked Lucy.

'Why, yes, I would. It will give this little lady time to feel independent.' He sat down at the table and Lucy switched on the percolator and fetched two mugs. The kitten went to sleep in the curve of his arm and when they got up to go Mrs Simpkins took no notice at all. Lucy, a soft-hearted girl, heaved a sigh of relief. 'Do you suppose they'll miss each other?'

'Perhaps, but not with grief; in the wild once a young animal is able to fend for itself it becomes independent. Mrs Simpkins still has three kittens and this young lady will have Thomas and Mrs Trump to spoil her.'

They got into the car and he transferred the kitten to her lap while he drove. At his house he took her straight through the hall and into the kitchen where Mrs Trump was standing at the table beating something in a bowl while Trump sat in a chair by the Aga, reading the paper. Thomas sat at his feet and all three of them looked up as they went in.

Trump got to his feet and Mrs Trump paused in her beating.

'Your kitten, Mrs Trump,' said the doctor, and sat the little creature down beside Thomas, who stared in amazement while the kitten sniffed delicately at her fur and then curled up beside her.

'Well, I never did!' exclaimed Mrs Trump. 'Look at the little darling and my Thomas, taken an instant liking to each other.'

'Highly satisfactory,' said the doctor. 'She'll need feeding four times a day for a week or two, Mrs Trump...'

'You leave that to me, sir, I'll give her just what's needed, and no going outside either.' She smiled at Lucy. 'The young lady will be here for lunch?'

'Yes, Mrs Trump.' He glanced at the kitchen clock. 'We had better go and have a drink in the drawing-room.' He took Lucy's arm and turned her round, whistled to the dogs who had gone to look at the kitten, and walked her through the door into the hall. They were only just in the drawing-room when the front door bell pealed.

Lucy, ushered across the room towards the brightly burning fire, heard Trump's voice mingled with that of a woman. Fiona, she felt sure, and turned to face the door, in time to see that lady make an entry.

'William, darling... I thought I'd get here first so that we could have ten minutes together.' She stopped as her eyes lighted upon Lucy. 'Oh, I had no idea...' She recovered immediately, kissed the doctor's cheek and went on, 'Lucy Lockitt, isn't it? From the orphanage? Has William taken pity upon you? Your parents are away, aren't they?'

'Hello,' said Lucy. 'They're in Turkey. I don't know if Dr Thurloe has taken pity, but he has invited me to lunch.'

She smiled charmingly. Her eyes, decided the doctor, watching her, looked like emeralds.

He said easily, 'Of course, you two know each other.' The doorbell rang once more and he went on, 'You know the Walters, Lucy...' They came into the room and Lucy was thankfully enveloped in their kindly warmth. She was answering their questions about her parents' plans when the last guest arrived. A colleague of the doctor's, the senior consultant surgeon at City Royal. A man of the doctor's age, already going grey and with a long thin face and a ready smile.

'You know everyone here,' said the doctor, 'but not Lucy Lockitt—her parents——'

'I know of them.' The man shook Lucy's hand as the doctor introduced him as Charles Hyde. 'I'm sorry my wife couldn't make it—you're her stand-in, I expect, and a very charming one, I must say.'

Lucy smiled and murmured. So that was why she had been invited—to make up numbers round the table. It was a pity she loved William so very deeply, otherwise she would have disliked him very much. Men! she thought, and curled a pretty lip.

Lunch, if it hadn't been for Fiona, would have been a delightful meal. The food was superb—lobster tartlets followed by roundels of lamb and finished off with a caramel mousse served with a coulis of raspberries, washed down by a Puligny Montrachet, a wine which Lucy found very pleasant. She knew very little about wines, but Mr Hyde, taking an appreciative sip, pronounced it to be a vintage white burgundy. 'Trust William to keep a good cellar,' he observed. 'Have you known him for long?'

'No,' Lucy replied, then added obscurely, 'Mother and Father are friends of the Walters.'

Mr Hyde glanced sideways at her composed face. 'Oh, quite. I expect you get tired of people asking you how you like working at the orphanage, but I have occasion to go there sometimes. A well-run place, I have always thought.'

'Oh, it is. But sad too—no mothers or fathers, or, if there are any, they don't want to know.'

He nodded. 'Sad indeed. You like children—babies?'

She smiled widely. 'Well, yes, I do, but I can't imagine anyone who didn't being able to work there.'

'We have four children of our own—they seem like an entire orphanage at times! Tell me, did you not wish to go to Turkey with your parents?'

'Well, no. You see, I'd not be of any use. I don't know enough about my father's work.'

Mrs Walter took possession of her after lunch so that she got no opportunity to speak to William even if she had wished to, for Fiona had stayed beside him, not only at the table, but afterwards as they sat around gossiping in the drawing-room. Presently Mrs Walter got up to go and the rest followed her, and when she offered Lucy a lift she accepted at once. It was obvious that Fiona wasn't going to leave with the rest of them, and when the doctor came over to her and offered to drive her home she said cheerfully, 'There's no need for you to bother, but thank you all the same. Mrs Walter will drop me off. Thank you for a delightful lunch.' She smiled too brightly; she wasn't going to concede defeat to the horrible Mrs Seymour, only retreat in good order, more determined than ever to have her dear William. Somehow; she had no idea how.

She refused the Walters' invitation to go back with them and spend the rest of the day, saying, without a grain of truth, that she was expecting a phone call from her mother.

'Isn't that a very long way to phone?' asked Mrs Walter.

'Mother hates writing letters so she rings up once a week instead.'

Lucy said goodbye and let herself into the house. There was the rest of the afternoon to get through, and the evening. She fed Mrs Simpkins and the kittens, switched on the TV and switched it off again, and instead went into the drawing-room, where she sat down at the piano and played all the more sentimental music she could call to mind. She played well and it suited her mood; a mixture of rage, unhappiness and a firm determination to marry William.

She was quite glad to go back to work on the Monday morning. Imogen and Pauline were both back again, and, although they were out most evenings, they slept at home and Lucy saw them briefly at breakfast most mornings. But she didn't see the doctor at all.

It was at the end of the week, as she got off the bus and started the short walk to her home, that she came face to face with a girl of her own age. 'Francesca!' She gave a small shriek of surprise and delight echoed by the other girl.

'Lucy, how lovely seeing you! You never answered my letter at Christmas—I'm actually on my way to see you.'

'You're here in London, on holiday?'

'Litrik is over here for a seminar. Heavens, isn't this fun?'

Lucy took her arm. 'Come for a quick chat; how long are you here?'

'We're going back in three days' time.'

'The babies? Are they here too?'

'Of course, and Nanny is with us. We're at the Connaught.'

They had reached the house and Lucy let them in and called to Alice, who came hurrying in to see who it was.

'Miss Fran—my goodness, it's years since I've seen you!' She eyed Fran's fashionable outfit. 'A real smart young lady too.' She smiled widely. 'I'll bring you both some coffee...'

'Tea, please,' they chorused, and took themselves into the drawing-room, to curl up on chairs and exchange news. They hadn't seen each other for some time, although they had been at school together for years, and after that had stayed with each other from time to time, but Francesca had begun to train as a nurse and gone to live with her three aunts who had discouraged, in the nicest way possible, too many young visitors to their home, so Fran and Lucy had seen less and less of each other even though they kept up a regular correspondence.

Over cups of tea they made up for not having seen each other for so long and presently Lucy said, 'You're happy, aren't you, Fran?'

'Yes. I can't imagine ever being happier. Lucy, why aren't you married? You're pretty and you must meet any number of men.' She put down her cup. 'There must be someone?'

'Yes, but he's not—not available. At least, I'm pretty sure he's not.'

'You're still at that orphanage you wrote about? Can you get some time off? Will you come and stay with us for a week or so? We'd love to have you. You might find a Dutchman as I did.'

'I've got some holidays due. I think I'd love to come Fran. Mother and Father are away, and Imogen and Pauline are out a lot. I'd love to see the babies too. Some time in the early summer perhaps?'

'Oh, sooner than that. Look, I must go or Litrik will worry. I'll ring you before we go back and fix a date. Do you work on Saturday?'

'Only in the mornings, I'm home by one o'clock.'

At the door Fran said gently, 'You look sad, Lucy. Do you love him very much?'

'Yes, however, I'll get over it. I'd love to come and see you, I might even find that Dutchman!'

They laughed together and Lucy stood at the open door and watched Fran walking away down the quiet street in search of a taxi. She looked so happy and content, and was beautifully dressed too—never a pretty girl, she had blossomed into a charming *jolie laide*.

'That's what love does to you,' said Lucy to the empty street.

*   *   *

The seminar was over and the learned gentlemen who had attended it were drifting away or stopping to talk to colleagues or friends. Dr Thurloe wandered unhurriedly towards the entrance, discussing a knotty problem with Litrik van Rijgen. They hadn't seen each other for some months, but ever since they had been at medical school at Edinburgh Royal Infirmary, and later at Cambridge and Leiden, they had kept in touch.

Litrik glanced at his watch. 'Fran's gone to see an old friend, she said she would be back at the hotel about six o'clock—we've time for a drink.'

The pub on the corner was shabby and awfully dark, but almost empty. They settled at a table in a corner and Dr Thurloe said, 'Well, that's over for another year. A pity you can't stay for a few days. Give my love to Fran, she looks marvellous and the babies are enchanting.'

His friend looked faintly smug. 'Fran's a wonderful wife and the children are delightful. Why not come back to the hotel, just for a half an hour, and say goodbye in person?'

Francesca was back by the time they arrived, lying on the floor of their sitting-room playing with the toddler's bricks, but she jumped up as they went in, greeted her husband as though they had been parted for weeks, held up his small son for a kiss and then turned to William, offering a cheek with the simplicity of a child. 'The baby's asleep,' she told them. 'Have you finished your papers?' She smiled at her husband. 'I've had a lovely time with Lucy, it was great to see her again. She's prettier than ever. I've invited her to stay, Litrik, you won't mind? She was getting off the bus and I was just walking up the road to her home. She's still at the orphanage.'

Dr Thurloe had been studying the baby in her carry-cot, but he turned round slowly as Fran spoke. 'Not by any chance Lucy Lockitt of nursery rhyme fame?'

'Yes—do you know her? She never said.' Francesca paused, a dozen likely and unlikely ideas in her head. 'We were at school together and we've kept in touch. I said I'd give her a ring before we go back home and settle a date. She said early summer; I'd like her to come before then.'

Dr Thurloe spoke casually. 'Give me a date, will you? I have the ear of the Matron at the orphanage.'

'Oh, splendid. Can you let me know before I phone Lucy, then she can ask—and get it,' she finished hopefully.

'I can't see why not. I'll give you a ring some time in the morning.' He smiled gently. 'I must be going—a dinner date.'

'Who with?' Fran blushed at his look and said, 'Sorry, it's none of my business.'

'A handsome lady of thirty-odd years, widowed, comfortably situated and well versed in the social graces.'

Francesca stretched up to kiss his cheek. 'Then don't let us keep you, she sounds just perfect.'

'What for?'

She gave him an innocent look. 'Why, a doctor's wife, of course. It's time you married, William.'

CHAPTER FIVE

LUCY went to the theatre with Pauline and Cyril on Saturday evening. It was something put on by an arts club in one of the smaller theatres and extremely highbrow. She gave up trying to understand what it was about halfway through the first act and allowed her thoughts to wander to William. He would be out, she guessed, dining and dancing probably. Her evening would have been much happier if she had known that he was miles away in the Cotswolds, spending his day with the old professor who had taught him so well in Edinburgh. She was taken to supper after the play ended, and listened to Cyril discussing the dialogue at length. The play had its merits, he informed them gravely, but he then went on to tear it to pieces.

'If you knew it was going to be so bad, why did we go?' asked Lucy.

'I was given tickets,' said Cyril huffily.

It was a pity they disliked each other, she thought, and agreed politely to being taken home before he and Pauline went back to his parents' house for the night.

She tactfully thanked him very nicely before she went indoors, where she kicked off her shoes, drank the cocoa Alice had ready for her, and went to bed. Pauline wouldn't be home until after office hours on Monday, but Imogen came in soon after she did and came along to her room to suggest that they might spend the next day in the country. 'Though I must be back soon after

six o'clock—I've got a dinner date. We could drive to
Epping—no, we'll go on to Ingatestone and have lunch
at that nice place. We haven't had a chance to gossip
for ages, have we?'

From which remark Lucy deduced that her sister had
something she wanted to tell her. 'It sounds lovely. What
time shall we go?'

'Oh, elevenish. Alice could have the day to herself after
breakfast.'

It was a bright morning when Lucy got up; March,
having come in rather noisily, had now become as quiet
as a lamb. She put on a jersey three-piece, with sensible
shoes, and went down to breakfast.

Traffic was thin as they drove east through London,
and it stayed that way until they reached Epping, although there were cars enough going towards the coast.
Imogen parked the car and led the way into the hotel
restaurant. 'We might go for a walk after lunch,' she
suggested. When she would be told whatever it was that
Imogen wanted her to know, decided Lucy, and took
care to keep the talk general as they ate lunch.

They had been walking for ten minutes or so, saying
nothing much, when Imogen said abruptly, 'I'm going
to be married, Lucy.'

It was a surprise: Imogen, at twenty-eight, had already made her mark in the business world, she had a
big salary, she was thought much of by her boss, and
her future as an executive was assured. She knew her
own worth and had never hesitated to let her family know
that, and somehow they had all thought of her as staying
single.

'Imogen, what a lovely piece of news! Who is he? Do
Mother and Father know?'

'I cabled them yesterday. Of course, we shall wait until they're back home before we marry. You don't know him—he's a Canadian businessman, George Irwell.'

'I hope you'll be very happy,' Lucy said, and meant it. 'You'll be married before Pauline and Cyril.'

'Yes. I'm the eldest anyway... and what about you Lucy? Haven't you met anyone you would like to marry?' She didn't give Lucy a chance to answer. 'I suppose not, buried at that orphanage of yours. Such a pity, for you're pretty enough, only you don't bother much, do you?' She laughed, and added without meaning to be unkind, 'Mother has always said that you're the home-bird, whatever that means.'

A prospect Lucy didn't care to contemplate. It was a sobering thought which remained with her for the rest of the day, and she was quite glad when Monday morning came round again.

She was halfway through the morning when Matron sent for her.

'I don't want to hassle you, but would you care to take a couple of weeks' holiday in a week or two's time? There will be no one else on holiday and we can cover for you. You have always been very accommodating about fitting in with the rest of us. Any time in March or April will suit me; at a pinch we could manage the first week in May. Will you think it over and let me know?'

Lucy went back to Miranda and set about giving her her midday dinner while she thought about holidays. Fran had asked her to stay, but she remembered that she herself had suggested the early summer, so Fran might not be prepared to have her earlier than that. It was a pity, for if she took two weeks' holiday within the next few weeks she could hardly expect to get more time off before the autumn, especially as the other girls had their plans already made. She finished her day undecided what to do, aware that she would have to make up her mind before she saw Matron again.

As it happened, her mind was made up for her that very evening.

Both her sisters were out, Imogen with her George, Pauline with Cyril. Lucy had eaten her supper in the kitchen with Alice for company, and then wandered away to wash her hair. Only before she could do that the phone rang. It was Francesca.

'Lucy, we're leaving this evening in about an hour. Look, couldn't you manage to come and stay with us before the summer? Surely you could get a couple of weeks off soon?'

'As a matter of fact, Matron asked me this morning if I'd mind taking two weeks either at the end of this month or in April.'

'Oh, good. Then you'll come; when?'

Lucy suddenly felt excited. 'Wait while I get a calendar. How about the last week in March, that's only a week away? You're sure——?'

'Don't be silly, of course I'm sure. Let's see, that will be the twenty-fifth on a Saturday. Litrik'll meet you at Schiphol; let us know the time the flight arrives when you've got everything fixed up. It'll be such fun, Lucy, there are years of gossip to catch up on. I must fly— Litrik's got the car waiting. See you.'

Fran put down the phone and smiled at her husband. 'That's settled. How clever of William to get round that matron. I wonder why he did. Do you suppose he fancies Lucy?'

'My darling, William is a kind man; I dare say he thinks that Lucy needs a holiday and he was able to make things easy for her.'

He smiled at her slowly and crossed the room to kiss her. Fran kissed him back. 'Is that so? They would make a very nice pair.' She frowned in thought. 'Do you suppose William might like to take a week or so's holiday and come and stay with us as well?'

'Matchmaker,' observed Litrik lovingly, and kissed her again. 'We shall miss that hovercraft.'

Lucy gave her holiday dates to Matron the next day, and when she got home that evening she told her sisters. They smiled at her with affection, remarked that it would be nice for her to have a holiday, and fell to the much more important task of making wedding arrangements. Lucy hadn't expected them to take much interest in such an ordinary happening as a couple of weeks' holiday; she went along to the kitchen and told Alice, who responded with all the warmth her sisters lacked.

'Now that'll be nice,' said Alice, 'and you be sure and take some pretty clothes with you, Miss Lucy; you never know, Mr Right might be waiting for you in Holland. Not that I set much store by foreigners.'

'Francesca married one,' Lucy pointed out, and ate one of the cheese tartlets Alice had just taken from the oven. 'She thinks he's absolutely marvellous.'

'Quite right and proper too,' said Alice, 'since 'e's 'er 'usband.' She whisked the tray of tartlets out of reach. 'You'll have no supper if you eat them now,' she threatened. 'There's grilled sole and spinach and no potatoes—Miss Imogen says she must lose half a stone before the wedding.'

'In that case,' said Lucy, reaching for the tartlets, 'I'd better have another of these, dear Alice.'

She spent the rest of the evening listening to her sisters tossing ideas to and fro; receptions, bridesmaids, which church and the best places for honeymoons were discussed in depth. They paused presently and looked at her. 'You'll be a bridesmaid, Lucy,' said Imogen. 'Pink taffeta and flower wreaths, I think...'

Pauline had other ideas. 'I'll have four attendants, I think—you, of course, Lucy. I don't think Cyril can manage any free time before July. Sea-green, I think, with darker green sashes. The others will be Cyril's little nephew and his two nieces.'

Three tiresome children, reflected Lucy, who loved children, all excepting these three—spoilt, quarrelsome and tending to whine. When she had agreed pleasantly to everything that was suggested she took herself off to bed, to lie awake and think of William Thurloe and wonder where he was and what he was doing. She told herself crossly that she must try not to think about him quite so much; she was still determined to marry him, but when she did think about him it must be positively. Not useless longings which got her nowhere. She rearranged her pillows and began to plan her holiday wardrobe. She would buy some clothes... It was a pity William wouldn't be there to see them. Sleep overtook her before she could feel sad about it.

Her mother, apprised of the forthcoming holiday, said, 'How nice, darling,' and plunged into an enthusiastic account of her father's latest find, the remains of an iron pot—proof, if they had needed it, that the Hittites really had known about smelting. Only when she had passed on this interesting information did she comment happily upon Imogen's forthcoming marriage, adding the rider that Lucy must be looking forward to being a bridesmaid twice over. 'A nice change from those orphans,' she declared with a little laugh, 'and enjoy yourself with Francesca, dear. Such a nice, quiet girl, and not at all pretty. Yet she has made a splendid marriage from what you tell me. You must see what you can do while you're in Holland, darling.'

Lucy said, 'Yes, Mother.' She had no need to go to Holland; just down the road to Chiswick.

She booked her flight, found her passport, fetched travellers' cheques and embarked on a day's shopping. March so far had been warm and sunny with occasional bouts of pouring rain. Fran had told her to be sure and bring a raincoat with her and a woolly or two, 'And something pretty for the evenings—I've planned a party and we shall go out to dinner and perhaps a concert.' She had sounded quite excited over the phone, and Lucy, immensely cheered at the prospect of some social life, went off and bought two new party dresses as well as a thin woollen suit in which to travel.

Each day she had gone to the orphanage hoping to see Dr Thurloe, but she never did. Miranda was improving by leaps and bounds, but she wasn't due to go to the clinic for another two weeks, when Lucy would be in Holland, so she would miss a chance of seeing him then.

It was on her last day at the orphanage before she started her holiday that she met Fiona Seymour. It had been a busy day and she had hurried home, showered and changed and taken herself for a walk along the Embankment, to meet Fiona coming towards her, strolling along in a stunning outfit.

She stopped and Lucy perforce stopped too. 'My dear, you are the very last person I would expect to see. I thought you spent your days in the orphanage with those dreary children.'

'I work until five o'clock, and they're not dreary.' Aware that she had sounded snappy, Lucy added, 'It's a gorgeous evening, isn't it?'

'I suppose so, though I'm having to waste some of it. William—Dr Thurloe—was to drive me to Henley, I've a dreary aunt living there, but he phoned to say he has some emergency or other and he won't be able to take me. Luckily I have a number of other friends and no lack of offers to take his place, although I'm having to hang around until I can be called for. I got bored indoors.' She gave Lucy a quick rather malicious glance. 'William's upset, of course; we spend as much time as we possibly can together.'

Lucy racked her brains to find a suitable reply to this. 'He's a busy man,' she observed mildly.

'Of course, I suppose you see him occasionally with those precious orphans. It must be dire working with them, but I suppose if you haven't any prospect of marrying it's better than nothing.' She drew a breath and put up her hand to her mouth. 'Oh, my dear, that sounded awful! Do forgive me, I was only repeating what William said...'

Lucy had gone rather pale, but her voice was quite clear and steady and very quiet. 'It's most interesting, and I like children. I should hate to live the kind of life you do, although I dare say it takes up quite a lot of time, make-up and hair and so on, and dieting...' Her green eyes were like deep green pools, her smile charming. 'I must fly, I've so much to do before I go away. Bye.'

She isn't likely to repeat that to William, decided Lucy, walking home rather fast, and I know I was rude, but she was rude first. And if William really said that about me I'll never speak to him again. She bounced into the house with such vigour that Alice came from the kitchen to see what was the matter.

'There you are, Miss Lucy. A pity you were out, that nice Dr Thurloe phoned to wish you a happy holiday—heard you were going from your matron, he said. I asked him to ring back, but he said he was going out.'

'Oh, he is, is he?' uttered Lucy rather wildly. 'As though I care what he does.'

She pounded upstairs to her room and Alice went back to the kitchen. 'So that's the way the wind blows,' she observed to Mrs Simpkins. 'We'll just have to wait and see, won't we?'

Mrs Simpkins, cleaning her whiskers after her tea, merely stared and yawned.

Right at the back of Lucy's head had been the idea that Dr Thurloe might phone again before she left, but the telephone remained silent and she started on her journey to Heathrow, speeded on her way by Alice and determinedly taking care not to look round in case the doctor, at the very last minute, should appear. Of course, he didn't, and she took herself through the routine at the airport and in due course boarded her plane.

She had met Litrik van Rijgen only twice before, at his wedding to Fran and during a visit they had paid to London just before the first baby had been born. When she saw him waiting for her at Schiphol she thought that he hadn't changed at all. He was a big man with greying fair hair and a handsome face, which in repose looked severe, although, reflected Lucy as she went towards him, it was unlikely that he was, for Francesca adored him and, as far as Lucy could discover from her letters, he made her blissfully happy. He saw her then, and smiled as he strode towards her.

'How very nice to see you again, Lucy.' He bent and kissed her cheek. 'Fran is so looking forward to your visit—so am I. Is this all your luggage?'

He led the way out of the airport and ushered her into the silver-grey Daimler parked close by. 'We shall be home in about half an hour—it is about thirty miles, just the other side of Utrecht. You had a comfortable flight?'

She found him a very likeable man, and they talked comfortably together as he drove until he turned off the motorway and joined a country road, which was very peaceful after the rush of traffic on the motorway. The village they reached was small and dominated by a large church, and a hundred yards further on Litrik swept the car between brick pillars and along a drive bordered by shrubs and trees, rounded a curve and drew up before his home.

It was a solid flat-faced house with orderly rows of windows, each with shutters. The house door was reached by way of circular steps and was solid enough to withstand a siege. It was opened now by a thin elderly man and Francesca flew past him and down the steps, to receive a quick embrace from her husband before she flung herself at Lucy.

'Oh, isn't this fun! Come in . . .' She flashed a smile at Litrik and took Lucy's arm. 'Are you tired? Did you have a good trip? We'll have lunch in half an hour or so.' She called over her shoulder, 'You won't be long, darling?'

Litrik smiled at her and Lucy, watching them, felt envious of such quiet happiness. 'Five minutes, love.'

'This is Trugg,' said Fran, and waited while Lucy shook hands with him. 'He's our right hand. Come up to your room and I'll leave you for a few minutes to tidy if you want to.'

She led the way up the wide staircase to the gallery above the hall and opened a door. 'Here you are, Lucy; the bathroom's through that door, and if you want anything just ask, won't you?'

She dropped a kiss on Lucy's cheek. 'This is fun, it really is. Come down when you're ready.'

Left to herself, Lucy explored the pretty room, admiring the mahogany furniture and the pretty sprigged chintz at the window and the thick matching bedspread. And the bathroom was quite perfect, pink and white and furnished with a pile of fluffy towels, bowls of soap and bath essences and a wide mirror, well lit. She went back into the bedroom and sat down before the triple mirror on the dressing table. She was a girl who almost always looked immaculate; she powdered her nose, put on more lipstick and brushed her hair, took a quick look at the garden from the window, and went down the staircase.

There were a number of doors in the hall and she paused uncertainly as Litrik flung a half-open door wide. 'We're in here having a drink,' he said and she went past him into the drawing-room.

It was a grand room, furnished most beautifully with antique pieces which gleamed with the patina of years of loving care, but there were great comfortable chairs too, and two enormous sofas, one on each side of the hooded fireplace. French windows opened on to a garden alive with spring flowers and a fire burned brightly. But its grandness was mitigated by all the signs of family living: a teddy bear leaning against a wall cabinet, a pile of knitting cast down on one of the lamp tables, a pile of magazines and newspapers on the sofa table, and before the fire two dogs, a mastiff and a much smaller dog, rather stout and with a long curly coat. They got up and came to sniff her and she put out a hand.

'Thor and Muff,' said Litrik. 'You like dogs?'

'Oh, yes, but we haven't one at home, only Mrs Simpkins the cat and her kittens.'

'Mrs Trugg has a cat—Moses—Litrik fished him out of the canal. There's a donkey too, in the paddock, and horses—Litrik has taught me to ride,' said Fran.

They sat around talking until Fran said, 'Shall we just peep at the children? Nanny will have fed them—baby has purée twice a day now, though I still feed her.'

The two of them went upstairs to the nursery where a miniature Litrik was perched in a high chair more or less feeding himself, while a young plump woman sat by him with the baby on her lap.

'This is Nanny,' said Fran. 'She was here before we married and I hope she'll never leave us.'

She sat down and took the baby on her lap while they watched little Litrik having the last of his dinner. 'They will rest now,' said Fran, 'and we have them until bathtime—Litrik isn't always home, of course, but he is marvellous with them. Wasn't it nice having a boy and then a girl? We want another pair—four makes a nice family.'

Lucy said wistfully, 'You must be so happy, Fran.' And then, in case she sounded self-pitying, 'They'll have a lovely home; it's so beautiful...'

'The garden's lovely in the summer, and the country around is pretty.' Fran got up and put the baby back in her cot and tucked her in carefully, dropped a kiss on her small son's head, said something to Nanny to make her smile, and suggested that they might go down to their own lunch.

'I say,' said Lucy, 'I suppose you speak Dutch?'

'Yes, but I make lots of mistakes still. Nanny understands some English, and of course Trugg is English, although Mrs Trugg, who cooks and housekeeps, only has a smattering.'

Lunch was a cheerful affair—there was so much to talk about and Litrik, Lucy decided, really was a very nice man. It was no wonder Fran was so happy. Almost as nice as William, Lucy admitted, a thought which made her ponder about him and, almost as though Fran knew it, she asked casually if Lucy went to the City Royal much and if she knew any of the staff there. She avoided her husband's amused eye as she did so, and appeared very nonchalant.

'Well, yes, I go sometimes to the clinics...' Lucy went a delicate pink. 'Some of the children aren't quite normal and they have to see a—a consultant.'

Such a vivid mental picture of William was imprinted behind her eyelids that for a moment she couldn't go on, and Litrik, apparently unnoticing of that, asked, 'Have they still got that out-of-date Outpatients there? As dark as a cellar, and it always smelled of damp clothes.'

A remark which led the conversation safely back to generalities.

The rest of the day passed pleasantly, Lucy playing with the children, being shown over the house and exploring the garden. In the evening, after one of Mrs Trugg's delicious dinners, they talked again; there was so much to say and, as Fran said, several years to catch up on.

Lucy, getting ready for bed, reflected on her evening. She had enjoyed it very much. Fran hadn't changed; she had beautiful clothes and an elegant hairstyle, but she was still kind-hearted, gentle Fran and Litrik loved her... 'And that is how I wish William would love me,' Lucy said to herself as she jumped into her very comfortable bed.

She woke once in the night, at a time when everything appeared to be at its blackest, convinced that she had no chance at all against the practised charms of Fiona Seymour. Fortunately when she awoke in the morning such a gloomy thought had no chance against daylight's common sense. She had as much chance as any other girl, she told herself stoutly, and sat up in bed to drink the morning tea that a nice cheerful girl had brought.

She was taken to church in the morning after a breakfast of hot rolls, ham and cheese and delicious coffee, and a quick visit to the nursery to see the children. Fran had been up early to feed the baby, and Litrik had been out with the dogs, and there was a pleasant air of bustle about the house.

The family pew was at the front of the church, under the pulpit with its vast sounding-board, and Lucy sat between Fran and Litrik, unable to understand a word, and yet following the service very well—some of the hymns even had tunes she knew. The sermon lasted a very long time, and the *dominee* thundered above her head so that she had the impression that he disliked his congregation, but as they left the church they stopped to speak to him and she discovered him to be a mild man with a splendid command of English and a soft, gentle voice.

He was very pleased to meet her, he said, and if she could spare the time he and his wife would be delighted to see her at his house. She thanked him nicely and Fran said, 'We'll walk down one day; I'm sure you'll have a lot to talk about. Have the children got over their measles?'

She was assured that they had, and they parted on the best of terms, to walk home and spend an hour in the nursery before having drinks and their own lunch. In the afternoon Litrik drove to the Veluwe, this time in a station-wagon with the dogs at the back and Lucy and Fran behind him each with a baby. It was a sunny day, but windy; he found a sheltered spot presently, and they all piled out, poking around the hedges for primroses, walking beside a narrow canal where a duck family was swimming. The hedges petered out very soon and the road ran, narrow and empty, towards the flat horizon, the country between dotted with farmhouses and villages, their church steeples dominating the field around them.

'Just where are we?' asked Lucy, no longer sure of the points of the compass.

'It all looks alike, doesn't it? We have driven through the Veluwe, and now we are on its very edge, back to the fields and flat country. The Veluwe is rather like your New Forest, only very much smaller. It's a great holiday area, and away from the road there are quite a few charming houses. Arnhem is to the south of us,' he waved a large arm, 'over there is Utrecht, and beyond but more to the north is Amsterdam. We'll take you there before you go back.'

They wandered back to the car and went home to tea round the fire, with Litrik's small son on his knee and the baby asleep in her Moses basket. Lucy sat, not talking much, soothed by the charming room and the gentle talk. She looked at the dogs and thought that, if she almost closed her eyes, she could fancy that they were Robinson and Friday and that Litrik was William.

The days flowed gently into a week; Lucy, getting ready for a bath and bed at the end of it, reviewed them. Each day there had been something different, and, even though Litrik had been away from home for a good deal of the day, Francesca had thought of something to do.

They had gone to Utrecht, inspected the great tower, poked around the shops, had coffee at the Café de Paris, decided against climbing the hundreds of steps of the Dom Tower, and returned home to take the children for a walk, accompanied by the dogs, until Litrik came home and friends came in for drinks. They had gone one evening to Litrik's parents' home and dined there with their other guests, and the next day Litrik had gone early to the hospital and come home again in time to drive them all up to Friesland to visit his great aunts, two formidable ladies who would never see eighty again, but who had lost none of their powers of command. Lucy had been taken on a tour of the house, which was old and furnished with heavy tables and chairs which looked as though they had taken root. They had ended up in the red salon, which had quite overpowered her.

'Frightful, isn't it?' Fran had said. 'I'd hate to live here, though I like Friesland. We visit from time to time. Litrik has a large family.' It had still been light when he'd left, and they had driven back across the Afsluitdijk, into Alkmaar, so that Lucy might see something of that town, to skirt Amsterdam and take the road through Hilversum and so home.

On another day they had driven along the narrow quiet road beside the River Vecht, admiring the lovely old houses with their grounds bordering the water, built by the rich merchants of the eighteenth century. And one evening there had been people to dinner, and all this interspersed with the gentle day's routine and hours spent with the children.

'You must go and see Keukenhof next week,' Fran had said. 'It's a glorious sight now, you couldn't have come at a better time.'

Lucy had been tired then, but, although her head was full of all the sights she had seen, there was still room to think of William.

'Out with Fiona, I suppose,' she mumbled as she dropped off.

Litrik had Sunday free, he had said on the previous evening, and, sitting up in bed, drinking her morning tea, Lucy wondered what pleasures were in store for her. The maid had pulled the curtains back and the sky was blue, the sun was shining and there didn't seem to be too much wind. Lucy hopped out of bed, flung up the window and hung out to enjoy the expanse of velvety lawn and the flower-beds filled with tulips and hyacinths. The birds were singing too, and the sun held warmth.

'Come gentle spring, ethereal Mildness, come,' carolled Lucy from her window, just as the peace of the garden was broken. Litrik was coming round the corner of his house, the dogs with him, and, strolling beside him, his hands in his pockets, looking very much at home, was William.

She stared down at him, unable to believe her eyes, her mouth open while happiness almost choked her. The two men looked up then, and Litrik said pleasantly, 'Oh, good morning, Lucy. I think you know William? He's an old friend, come to spend a few days with us. Come on down and meet him.'

Lucy went on staring with nothing to say, and then a wide smile curved her mouth. 'Good morning,' she said in a wispy voice. 'I'll be down——' It struck her suddenly that she was hardly suitably dressed for a chat, and she withdrew her person smartly, only to poke her head out again, her hair in a tangle round her shoulders. 'Is Fiona with you?' she asked.

If Dr Thurloe was surprised, nothing of it showed on his placid face as he looked up at her. 'No, I'm alone.'

She nodded, still smiling, and shut the window, to dance across the room to the bathroom. While she showered she thought about what she would wear. It was still cool, although the sun shone and it was April. It had better be the jersey dress. She dressed rapidly, brushed her hair to shining smoothness, applied lipstick and raced downstairs.

The two men were coming out of Litrik's study as she reached the hall, and she went to meet them, quite unaware of the delight on her face. Indeed, she might have uttered a good deal which she would have regretted later if it hadn't been for Fran running down the staircase after her, calling out as she came, 'William—how delightful! Of course, you'll stay? And it won't be just babies and us...' She gave a well-simulated start of surprise. 'Oh, do you two know each other?'

She leaned up to give William a kiss and he said gravely, 'We have met—at the clinic and various dinner parties.'

'Oh, isn't it a small world?' Fran declared and both men agreed with a blandness which belied the gleam in their eyes.

But Lucy hadn't noticed, and she said now, rather shyly, 'It does seem strange meeting here. Are you on holiday?' And, in case he should think that she was prying, 'I am, I've been here a week already. I knew Fran at school.'

'There's nothing like old friends,' observed Dr Thurloe easily. 'How are you liking Holland?'

They went in to breakfast and Lucy, the seething of her feelings settling down under his casual friendliness, joined in the light-hearted talk.

Fran, pouring coffee, asked half laughingly, 'And how is that handsome lady of thirty-odd years—the comfortably situated widow with the social graces? You were going to take her out...?'

The doctor's eyes were on Lucy's face. 'Fiona Seymour? As handsome as ever. You must meet her next time that you come over, and see for yourself.'

Lucy buttered a roll and didn't look up. She said evenly, 'She dresses beautifully, Fran, and always in the right clothes, if you know what I mean.'

She looked up then, straight at William, and smiled at him. It was the kind of smile Boadicea might have had on her face as she led the Iceni into battle. He stared back at her; she was in a temper despite the smile, and her eyes sparkled like emeralds.

He said mildly, 'I suppose that matters to women; I don't think men notice such things.' He smiled gently. 'At least, only upon occasion.'

Lucy went slowly a very pretty pink, remembering that there had been far too much of her hanging out of her bedroom window. Just for the moment she could think of nothing crushing to say; when she did, she would say it.

CHAPTER SIX

SINCE it was Sunday, they all went to church and Lucy, sitting with Fran on one side of her making sure she could follow the service, was very conscious of William's bulk on her other side. She stood up and sat down just as she should, but she didn't understand a word thundered at her from the pulpit and, although she opened her hymn book obediently at Fran's direction, she had no idea of what they were singing. She was wondering how it was that Fran had heard about Fiona; William must have said something, but when? She sat there frowning until she was gently prodded to her feet for the final hymn.

They stayed talking to the *dominee* for quite a while after the service and then Litrik and William walked on ahead, leaving her and Fran to follow. They had a lot to talk about, and William wasn't mentioned.

Nanny was in the garden playing ball with little Litrik while the baby slept in her pram.

'Go and have your coffee, Nanny,' said Fran, 'and will you ask someone to bring ours out here? We'll stay with the children.'

The two men began a gentle game of ball with the little boy staggering happily between them, and Fran and Lucy went to sit by the pram. The baby was charming, pink and white and fair-haired. Lucy bent over her and murmured, 'She's beautiful, Fran, and she has such a pretty name.'

'Lisa—I asked Litrik if I could tell you about that and he said that he'd like you to know. You see, when I first met him he had a ward, a little girl with spina bifida. Her father had died—he was a friend of Litrik's—and her mother left her. So he became her guardian until she died soon after we married. She was a darling and we still miss her.'

She smiled rather mistily at Lucy, who thought, looking at her friend's expressive face, that there was a lot more to the story than that, but all she said was, 'Thank you for telling me, Fran. Little Lisa will fill her place . . .'

Trugg had put the coffee-tray on the garden table and they sat around drinking and making vague plans for the week ahead.

'You two girls can do what you like tomorrow,' said Litrik. 'William will come with me to Utrecht; we shan't be back until the early evening. There's the party on Wednesday, isn't there, darling? And on Thursday I've arranged to be free and we might all go to Keukenhof.'

Sunday lunch was a leisurely affair, and afterwards—she wasn't quite sure how it happened—Lucy found herself walking briskly out of the gate beside William.

'A good walk, just what we need after that magnificent meal,' he observed.

'I don't remember saying that I wanted to come.'

'My dear girl, where is your tact? I'm sure that Litrik and Fran would like an hour or two on their own—he's a busy man, you know, and he doesn't see as much of her or the children as he would wish.'

'Oh, well—I hadn't thought of that . . .'

'He loves his work, you know.'

They were walking along a narrow lane leading, as far as Lucy could see, nowhere at all. 'Do you love your work too?'

'Yes, and even when I marry it will still be a large part of my life,' he looked down at her, 'however much I love my wife and children.'

'You have children round you every day for hours—in the clinics and the wards, and I suppose at your consulting rooms. And then you'll go home to them?' She frowned a little thinking that Fiona, if she had children, would keep them out of the way with a nanny—they'd be in bed by the time he got home. There would be guests for dinner and Fiona waiting for him in some exquisite outfit...

'Now what are you dreaming up?' asked William. 'I suspect you have far too much imagination. If you are worried as to my future, don't be—I have it all nicely planned.'

Lucy stopped to admire the view, a gentle rise and fall of endless fields with a farmhouse here and there and cows in abundance. There was a farm cart coming towards them too, drawn by a great horse, plodding patiently. They stood aside to allow it to pass and William exchanged unintelligible greetings with the driver. Only when it had gone did she speak.

'I am not in the least worried about your future,' she told him coldly. 'Why should I be? Nor do I need to draw on my imagination about it, for it is a foregone conclusion, isn't it?'

He looked interested. 'Oh, is it? May I know?'

She said, still coldly, 'Why should I tell you something you already know?'

He said blandly, 'I believe we are at cross purposes. Never mind, time enough for that ... I saw in the *Daily Telegraph* that Imogen has become engaged. Does she plan to marry before Pauline? And when do your parents return?'

The rest of their walk was taken up with what Lucy considered to be pointless chat. She returned to the house in quite a nasty temper, although she was too well brought up to show it. But she couldn't conceal the vivid green of her eyes. The doctor was quick to see that and smiled to himself.

The men left early the next morning, and after an hour or more in the nursery Fran got into her car and, with Lucy beside her, drove to Arnhem, where they spent the rest of the morning wandering round the open air museum with its replicas of old cottages, windmills and farms from a bygone age. 'You see,' explained Fran, 'there's not time to take you all over Holland, and here you get an idea of the history of each province. I wish you could stay another week, Lucy.'

'So do I, but I have to be back because one of the other helpers is going on holiday. There are never enough of us anyway.'

They had their coffee at the Rijzenburg Restaurant, a few miles out of Arnhem and, since it was almost lunchtime, ordered omelettes and salads at the same time. 'Though I must be back by two o'clock to feed the baby,' said Fran. 'Do you think I should spend more time with the children? Of course, when there's no one visiting, I'm with them almost all day.'

'I think you're a marvellous mother,' declared Lucy, 'and I think you must be a jolly good wife too.'

'Oh, good. I'm very happy, you know—I hope you find the right man, Lucy; being married is such fun.' She looked across the table at her friend. 'But there is someone, isn't there?'

Lucy went pink. 'Yes. But he doesn't know and I don't suppose he ever will, for I won't tell him.'

Fran said gently, 'Think about it, often things have a way of turning out well. Don't ever give up hope, Lucy.' She glanced at her watch. 'Heavens, we'd better go.'

Later that afternoon they took the children for a walk, with Lisa in her pram and little Litrik on his reins, and after that it was nursery tea and the fun of bathtime. The men came home then, and Nanny went away to have her supper while the four of them saw the little ones into their cots. There was a good deal of laughter and squeals of delight from the little boy, but presently he sat on his father's knee while his evening quota of nursery rhymes were recited and baby Lisa went to sleep at once.

With Nanny back, they went to tidy themselves for the evening and presently met again in the drawing-room to discuss the day's events. The two men had been busy, although they only touched lightly on their work. Lucy had the impression that if she hadn't been there Litrik would have gone into details, for it was obvious that Fran knew exactly what he was talking about and was interested too. She allowed her thoughts to wander presently, trying to picture Fiona listening to William when he got home with just such a look of rapt attention on her face as Fran had. But the picture refused to take shape; Fiona wouldn't want to know, she would give him a drink and tell him who was coming to dinner.

She stole a quick look at him, sitting at his ease, a glass in his hand, content after his day. And that was how it should be every evening, she reflected, and how it would be if only she could marry him. It would be so helpful if Fiona could meet a very rich man who liked her lifestyle. She looked up and found the doctor's eyes on her, and just for a moment she couldn't look away, unaware that her dreams were in her face.

He smiled slowly. 'Will you come to Amsterdam with me tomorrow, Lucy?'

She nodded. 'I'd like that very much, thank you. I expect you've been there before?'

He nodded. 'But it's a place where you can go back time and again and each time find something new. We shan't be able to see everything, but we'll pack in as much as we can.' He looked across the room to Fran. 'Will it be all right if we go directly after breakfast, Fran?'

'Of course, and come back here when you like. If you decide to stay out to dinner, just give us a ring. Are you going to the hospital again before you go back?'

'Wednesday...'

'But don't forget the party. About a dozen for dinner, and hordes coming afterwards.' She got up and went to sit by Lucy. 'What are you going to wear?'

It was a doubtful kind of morning when Lucy woke, and her suit seemed the most suitable thing to wear; if it rained it would afford some protection, and if it turned fine it would be just right for the time of year. She dressed with care, pinned up her hair into a french pleat, got into low-heeled shoes—for there was no knowing where William might take it into his head to go—and went down to breakfast.

They left directly that meal was over, and since Amsterdam was a mere twenty-five or so miles away they were there in just over half an hour. The inner city appeared to be jammed with cars, parked on either side of the numerous canals and wherever there was an inch of room on the narrow streets. But William drove straight on and presently turned into the forecourt of a hospital. 'I know the *Directeur*,' he said casually. 'We can park here for as long as we like.'

Which he did with a minimum of fuss before taking Lucy's arm and walking her out into the busy street. 'Coffee first,' he suggested, and crossed the road and plunged down a narrow alleyway which brought them out into a tree-lined street, teeming with people and traffic and lined with cafés and smart boutiques. They sat at a table on the pavement and drank their coffee, watching the passers-by while the doctor explained the lay-out of the city. 'Think of a spider's web,' he observed. 'The circular threads are the canals intersected by streets and alleys. Shall we walk first before we go on the canals?'

He knew his way very well, and they wandered in and out of narrow streets, across small, arched bridges, alongside the canals, admiring the patrician houses with their great front doors reached by double steps, their high windows and their gables, each one slightly different from its neighbours.

'What are they like inside?' wondered Lucy aloud.

'Delightful. Amazingly well modernised without spoiling their original charm. I've been in several—Litrik is old friends with some of the professors at the hospitals in the city. Two of them are married to English girls, I believe there are more than that number. Fran could tell you; she visits them from time to time.'

He led her into a narrow cobbled street lined with little antique shops and waited patiently while she peered into their windows. Before walking back to the Dam Square, they went along Damrak and so to where the canal tours started. The boat they took wasn't very full, and the guide's voice was easy to follow because everything was repeated in English and French. When it was over and they were back on dry land Lucy said, 'That was marvellous; I must try and remember it all...'

'Well, you can always refresh your memory—it is only a couple of hours from home, you know.'

He beckoned a taxi and popped her into it. 'Lunch,' he said.

He took her to Dikker and Thijs in which elegant restaurant they ate a delicious lunch; onion tarts, grilled sole with tiny new potatoes and green peas, and, for Lucy, an enormous ice-cream smothered in whipped cream and chocolate sauce, while the doctor enjoyed a selection from the cheese board, and since they had the afternoon before them they drank sparingly from the hock he had ordered. Over coffee he made his suggestions for the afternoon.

The Rijksmuseum for a start, because when she got home everyone would expect her to have been there. 'The Begijnhof,' he went on. 'It's just off Spui, not too far from here. A circle of charming little houses where nuns once lived; the church in the centre is used for English Services. Then Rembrandt's house, and that, I think, is about all we can manage this time.'

'Oh, yes—it's very kind of you to take me round. I should never have seen all this on my own, and even if I never come again...'

He opened his eyes wide and their blue stare sent her heart thudding. 'But of course you will come again.'

He sounded so sure of that she didn't like to argue about it.

The afternoon was a kaleidoscope of old houses, famous paintings and exquisite silver and porcelain, all delightfully jumbled in Lucy's head so that sorting them out was going to take her quite a time.

'What a heavenly day,' she sighed happily, pouring tea. He had taken her to the Amstel Hotel, a fitting end to the day, for it was overlooking the Amstel with the barges going to and fro and an everchanging scene. She found it a delightful place, old-fashioned and solid and very elegant.

They took a taxi back to the hospital, got into the car and drove away from the city through solid traffic which at times hardly moved. But once on the motorway, William allowed the car to rush ahead, and it was still not yet seven o'clock as he stopped in front of the house.

Trugg admitted them with the hope that they had had a nice day, and begged them to go up to the nursery as Mevrouw was putting the children to bed. They left their outdoor things in the hall and went upstairs, to find Fran and Nanny bathing the children, a leisurely business entailing a good deal of splashing and childish shouting. They were joined within minutes by Litrik, and it was another half-hour before the children were tucked up for the night. The four of them dispersed to make themselves presentable for the evening, and presently foregathered in the drawing-room for drinks and to exchange news of their days. After dinner the two men went off to Litrik's study and the two girls spent the next hour or so checking the plans for the party.

'Do you plan to do anything in the morning?' asked Fran.

'No, I'd like to help you, if you need help.'

'Oh, good. The flowers—this is such a big house it takes all day just to do the downstairs rooms. Old Jan will bring in the pot-plants from the greenhouse, so if you could dot them around... He'll leave them in the garden-room beside the kitchen. The men will be out all day, which means we will be able to get on with everything. All Litrik's family will be coming, and his friends from the hospital and from Leiden too—there'll be about fifty of us, but only a dozen for dinner.'

Lucy said thoughtfully, 'You know, Fran, you haven't changed a bit—not you, that is, but you've taken to all this——' she waved expressively with her arms '—like a duck to water. Was it very difficult?'

Fran shook her head. 'No, you see, Litrik helped me, and Trugg and all the people who work here are quite marvellous, and I've a wonderful mother-in-law.' She went on casually, 'Has William got a mother and father?'

'I haven't an idea. We—we have only met occasionally. I had lunch at his home once—one Sunday with some of his friends. In fact, I only know that he has two dogs and a devoted housekeeper.'

'Well, he'd certainly need that; Litrik says he works a great deal harder than he should.' Fran smiled to herself. 'Litrik works too hard as well, but I nag him before it gets too bad.'

The next day passed pleasantly. In the morning Lucy was busy arranging the flowers here and there, and making herself useful running to and fro with Nanny, giving a helping hand with the children, and in the afternoon she washed her hair, did her nails and experimented with make-up. The men came home soon after tea, and the next hour was spent in the nursery before they went downstairs for a drink before going to dress.

Lucy, studying her image in the pier-glass in her room, hoped that William would find her worth a second glance, and, indeed, she looked charming. She had put on a new dress, amber silk with a long, full skirt, long tight sleeves and a ruched chiffon bodice and, excepting a thick gold chain, she wore no jewellery. She had allowed her hair to curl around her neck and, on second thoughts, hadn't used more make-up than usual. Nothing out of the ordinary, she decided, surveying her person with an eagle eye, and if Fiona Seymour were to have been among the guests Lucy would have stood no chance at all. She went downstairs and found Fran, very stylish in blue velvet, and Litrik correct in his black tie, sitting in the drawing-room, holding hands.

Litrik got up as she went in and said cheerfully, 'Drinks all round, I think, to get us in the mood.'

A moment later William joined them, the epitome of the well-dressed man at a party. He admired Fran and went to stand in front of Lucy. 'Charming,' he said, then added wickedly, 'Did it take all day?'

'Certainly not!' she retorted. 'I've been busy doing the flowers and playing with the children and running errands.' She gave an indignant snort. 'A good deal busier than you, I dare say.'

He smiled. 'Probably.' If he had been about to say more, there was no chance, for the first of the guests were arriving.

Lucy, after hopping into bed at two o'clock in the morning, lay wide awake just long enough to go over the evening. It had been tremendous fun; dinner had been a formal affair, the table appointments splendid, the food superb, and there had been no lack of enlivening conversation. She had sat between two cousins of Litrik's, both of whom had flirted with her in the nicest possible way; she had responded, hoping that William had noticed, but if he had his face remained blandly friendly and nothing more.

Presently, when the rest of the guests had arrived and they had all gone into the drawing-room, which had been cleared for dancing and with its double doors opening on to the covered veranda, she had been swept away to dance without a break. It was just as Trugg had announced that a buffet supper was being served in the dining-room that the doctor had appeared beside her.

'You're enjoying yourself.' It wasn't a question but a statement of fact. 'Let me get you something to eat before you disappear on to the dance-floor again.'

Lucy had made some casual answer, discomfited by the thought that he hadn't made any effort to dance with her. Not that she could blame him—there had been any number of pretty girls there, and he had danced with almost all of them. And, to make matters worse, they had joined a party at one of the bigger tables and, although he sat next to her, he'd made no effort to talk to her other than in the general conversation all around them. It had pleased her enormously when one of her dance partners had got up finally and came to bend over her chair. 'Tear yourself away from that ice and come and dance, Lucy. It's a waltz and I'm feeling romantic.'

She had got to her feet at once, smiling at him, allowing William the tail-end of a smile before she had gone back to the drawing-room. And she had danced every dance after that, with the *burgermeester*, the *dominee*, a selection of young men whose names she couldn't remember, and Litrik. It wasn't until the band had been striking up for the last dance that William had appeared beside her once more, swept her into his arms and danced her away. It had been a waltz and he'd danced well, and just for a moment she'd forgotten that he had ignored her for most of the evening, that he would probably marry Fiona, that when they got back to England she might not see him again for several weeks; she had been happy, floating round the vast room, her cheek pressed to his shirt-front, his arm around her. She could have gone on forever, but of course she hadn't. The music had ended in a final flourish and the party had been over. Perhaps, she thought sleepily, she could change her style, tint her hair, buy clothes in the forefront of fashion and not just those which suited her, do something really clever so that he would notice her— even accompany her father on his next excavation. She just had time to reject this last plan before she fell asleep.

She was awake again by eight o'clock and out of bed to see what kind of a morning it was. They were to go to Keukenhof and if only it were a fine day she would be able to wear the deceptively simple Jaeger outfit she had been saving for just such an occasion.

The garden was bathed in early morning sunshine and looked beautiful, and as she looked she was aware of Litrik and William with the dogs. They were striding across the paddock beyond the grounds. She showered and dressed and went downstairs, just in time to see their broad backs disappearing through the front door, and Fran, her head peering round the door of the small room where they had breakfast, said, 'Aren't they gluttons for work? But they've promised faithfully to be back here by eleven o'clock to take us to Keukenhof.' She eyed

Lucy. 'I say, you do look smart, and just right for this kind of a day.' She opened the door wider. 'Come and have breakfast, and then help me bath the children; it's Nanny's morning off.'

Over breakfast Lucy asked, 'If it's Nanny's off-duty how can we go to Keukenhof?'

'She's coming with us. Twice a week she is free from half-past eight until half-past ten, so she takes the small car into Utrecht, has her hair done or shops, and so on. She likes it that way and it suits us very well.'

So the first part of the morning was spent in the nursery until Nanny came back and presently the men came home.

The party set off in two cars, Litrik with Fran, Nanny and the children, and William with Lucy—an arrangement which pleased her very well. Not easily disheartened, she was well aware that each time she spent with him gave her another chance to get him interested in her; so far she hadn't had much success, but she was a strong believer in kindly fate, although whether fate was going to be strong enough to overcome Fiona Seymour was a moot point.

They took the main road, circumventing Utrecht and, as they neared Amsterdam, turning south to Lisse. The Keukenhof gardens were just outside the town and, since it was a fine day, there were plenty of people strolling up and down the paths. They parked the cars, fastened little Litrik into his pushchair, tucked Lisa into her folding pram and set off. The flowers were a magnificent sight; huge beds of tulips, daffodils, hyacinths and still more tulips stretched as far as the eye could see. They wandered along for an hour or more and presently went to the restaurant, which was elegantly set among the background of trees and more flowers. They drank coffee and ate *broodjes* and little Litrik sat on his father's knee, eating his roll and gabbling away in a mixture of Dutch and English. And as for Lisa, good baby that she was, she slept peacefully in her pram.

There was still a great deal to see, and since Fran had said that they must go round the giant greenhouses so that she could order some plants for later on in the year they made their way there. 'I'll be ages making up my mind,' said Fran. 'William, you take Lucy with you and go at your own pace. We'll meet here at the entrance in half an hour or so, shall we? And if you're not ready by then we'll see you at the cars.'

The doctor proved to be a knowledgeable gardener, and, what was more, he ordered several boxes of bulbs for his own garden and then did the same for Lucy when she admired a particularly fine hyacinth. 'They send them over later,' he told her, and when she thanked him, 'Something to remind you of your stay in Holland.'

They were standing admiring a display of hothouse lilac when he observed placidly, 'Of course, you'll come back with me. So much easier in the car. I'll see about your ticket. I have to be home on Sunday, unfortunately—a dinner engagement I can't miss.' He glanced down at her, smiling a little. 'An important one I don't want to miss.'

She said stiffly, 'It's very kind of you to offer me a lift, but I can just as easily go by plane. I have my ticket...'

'Don't be tiresome, Lucy,' he said blandly. 'If you travel back with me there will be no need for Litrik to take you to Schiphol, and if we leave after breakfast on Saturday we'll be home for tea. I came by hovercraft.'

There was no point in arguing further; he was offering her a lift home out of consideration to his friends, and not because he wanted her company.

She said snappily, 'Very well, since it is convenient. Shall we go and find the others?'

'Tired of my company?' he asked silkily. And, before she could think of a suitable answer, 'That is an unfair question. You will either tell the truth or tell a pack of lies.'

'I am not in the habit of lying,' said Lucy haughtily.

'The truth wouldn't do either, would it?' he answered cheerfully.

At the cars he suggested that he might drive back to the house another way. 'So that Lucy can see a little more of Holland...' he explained, and Litrik agreed with him. 'A good idea. Take the road through Alphen aan de Rijn and Bodegraven. You can get a side-road from there which will take you north of Utrecht—you know the one I mean?—it weaves past the lakes and you can get to Bilthoven and Zeist. A peaceful, pleasant little run. You can get tea at Breukelen—there's a good hotel by the river, but come back to us if you don't feel like stopping.'

He smiled kindly at Lucy. 'You'll be quite safe with William; he knows this part of Holland almost as well as I do.'

He stowed his family carefully into his car, waved nonchalantly, and drove off.

Lucy got into William's car and sat silently until it occurred to her that he might think that she was sulking.

Conversation, polite conversation, that was, was imperative. 'You come to Holland quite often?' she wanted to know.

'Off and on. I'm an honorary consultant at Utrecht and Leiden, which means that I come over to lecture from time to time and also act as an examiner.' He gave her a quick sideways glance. 'Will you be sorry to go back home?'

'Yes, I think I shall. I've been happy here.' She could hardly add that that was because he had been there too. 'Fran is such a dear, and the babies are delightful. I like Litrik too.'

'A sound man. Fran is exactly right for him. I envy him—a wife, children and a lovely house that Fran has turned into a home...'

'You have a lovely house...'

'Indeed, yes. I really must add a wife and children as soon as possible.'

Lucy looked out of the window at the serene countryside. There was a potential wife waiting for him, wasn't there? Someone who would grace his table and manage his home to perfection. The children were another matter, but perhaps Fiona might change her mind... She said in a wooden voice, 'I hope you'll be very happy.'

He said placidly, 'I'm thirty-five and I've waited a long time for the right girl to come along. I know I— we shall be very happy.'

There seemed to be no answer to that. Lucy pointed out the sails of a boat apparently in the middle of a meadow and remarked on how interesting that was. He agreed gravely, 'The lakes are there—we shall turn off presently and you will have a better view. I think we might take Litrik's advice and have tea, don't you?'

A cup of tea was a panacea for all ills, she reminded herself, and agreed politely.

They stopped presently at a small, picturesque hotel by the water and sat watching the yachts gliding by in the quite stiff breeze while they drank their tea. Lucy, who had discovered that, contrary to the general idea, unrequited love had made no difference to her appetite, ate a mountainous cream cake with unselfconscious pleasure, watched, if only she had looked, by the doctor with amused tenderness.

They arrived back in good time to change for the evening and join Fran and Litrik for drinks before dinner. But before they went across the hall to the dining-room Fran said that she would just make sure the children were all right and Lucy went with her. They were both asleep, the baby's pale hair shining in the light of the small lamp near her cot, the little boy upside-down in his cot, clutching a teddy bear.

'Oh, Fran, you are lucky,' said Lucy softly, and in such a sad little voice that Fran looked at her.

'You'll be lucky too,' she said gently. 'I wonder what's round the corner for you.'

'The orphanage,' said Lucy bleakly. Nanny came from the day nursery then, and Fran stopped to speak to her, which Lucy thought was a good thing or she might have wallowed in self-pity.

She was very bright and chatty for the rest of the evening, something which puzzled all three of her companions, for she wasn't either bright or chatty by nature.

If she had been harbouring a secret hope that William might have plans to take her out on her last day, she was doomed to disappointment; at breakfast the two men were engrossed in their plans for the day—hospital rounds, an afternoon clinic, a visit to a retired professor and a meeting of consultants. There wasn't a minute to spare for anything or anyone else. They went off presently with the air of men well content with their world, and Fran took another slice of toast and poured more coffee for herself and Lucy. 'I thought we might go to Utrecht for a last look round,' she suggested. 'The men will be back soon after tea, so if you pack this afternoon we'll have a nice long evening with nothing to do. I shall miss you, Lucy.'

'I've loved being here, Fran. I'll remember these two weeks forever. And if I don't write often it's because I'm really quite busy...'

'I know, I shall phone you. Do you plan to stay at the orphanage?'

'I think so. I'm too old to train for anything, and besides, I'm not clever at exams and things like that. I took the job because I wanted to prove to Mother and Father that I could do something, and I really like my work.'

'You must come again, and I mean that.'

The pair of them spent the morning shopping, buying last-minute presents to take home and sweets for the orphans, and in the afternoon Lucy packed and put everything ready for going away in the morning. If she felt sad, nothing of that showed when the men came home. They sat round talking after dinner until late, and when she at last got into her bed Lucy was too tired to do more than give a long sigh before she slept.

They left after breakfast the next morning, with everyone standing on the steps to see them off. Amid cries of, 'See you again very soon,' and 'Have a good journey,' William drove out of the drive and into the lane on their journey back to England.

CHAPTER SEVEN

THE journey back to London was accomplished without a hitch and in comfort. The doctor drew up before Lucy's home at mid-afternoon, got out to unload her luggage, opened her door and then rang the doorbell. Alice welcomed them warmly, ushered them inside, suggested tea, and offered the news that neither Imogen or Pauline would be home until Sunday evening.

Anxious that William shouldn't feel obliged to offer her entertainment, Lucy said hastily, 'Oh, good, I could do with a day to sort things out on my own.' She added, rather belatedly, her invitation to have some tea before he went on to his own house, and, when he refused smilingly, she thanked him for her lift back, saying politely, 'I hope you have a nice evening.'

He didn't answer that, only smiled a little. 'I dare say we shall see each other from time to time,' he observed in a non-committal manner. 'Miranda will still need to visit me and you will probably be with her.'

She nodded and managed a smile, engulfed in a bitter disappointment that he had no plans to see her again unless it was at the clinic. And when he wished her goodbye a few moments later she made some inane remark about their holiday which, upon reflection, made no sense at all, but at least bridged the awkward gap between his goodbyes and departure. She stood on the doorstep and waved gaily as he drove away, and then went indoors and burst into tears.

'Things are never as bad as they seem,' said Alice, and gave her a motherly hug. 'You sit down and drink your tea and have a good cry if you want to, and then tell me all about your holiday.'

So Lucy sat down at the kitchen table with Mrs Simpkins on her lap and presently mopped her eyes, drank her tea and launched into an account of her two weeks in Holland. If there was a singular lack of information about the doctor, Alice didn't comment upon it. Instead she said briskly, 'You've 'ad two lovely weeks, Miss Lucy, and just you remember that. And now go and wash your face and telephone that nice Miss Fran and let her know you're back 'ome. And there's a note for you in the drawing-room from your sisters.'

'Is there a letter from Mother?'

Alice shook her head. 'I dare say she'll phone now you're back home.'

Lucy went upstairs taking her sisters' note with her. It bore out Alice's message that they wouldn't be at home until the following evening, and, beyond a vague hope that she had enjoyed herself, it was entirely taken up with their own doings.

Lucy read it twice and then went to look at her blotched face in the looking-glass. 'I should dearly love to wallow in self-pity,' she told her reflection, 'but a lot of good that would do. I shall plan a campaign.'

Alice had made a chicken casserole and followed it with one of her apple tarts, and over their meal Lucy discussed the forthcoming weddings, speculated over the dresses she would be expected to wear as bridesmaid, and observed that she was quite looking forward to going back to the orphanage. When she had helped Alice with the washing up, she declared herself tired after her journey and said goodnight. 'And I'll phone Fran before I go upstairs,' she told her old friend.

'Did you have a good trip?' Fran wanted to know. 'I hope William gave you a meal, you left so early.'

'We stopped on the way—just before we went on the hovercraft—and had an early lunch. We were back here in good time for tea.'

'Did you go out to dinner?'

'Well, no—William had a dinner engagement and I'm really quite tired.'

They gossiped for a few minutes more before Lucy rang off with the promise of a phone call later in the week.

Fran put the receiver down at her end and went back to sit by Litrik. 'I thought that there was something between William and Lucy,' she told her husband. 'He took her home, but he had a dinner engagement—I mean, if he was keen he would have asked her out... Do you suppose I've made a mistake, darling?'

Litrik lowered his newspaper. 'No, my love, but these things can't be hurried, you know. Lucy has a bee in her bonnet about this woman Fiona, and William, unless I am much mistaken, is holding back for a number of reasons. Give them time.'

'But they never see each other,' almost wailed Fran.

'My dearest, if William wants to see Lucy, he'll contrive to do so, be assured of that.'

Lucy spent Sunday sorting out her clothes, washing her hair, doing her nails and then going for a brisk walk along the Embankment, and if she was lonely after the cheerful company she had been in, she didn't admit it.

Everyone was glad to see her back on Monday morning, not least Miranda, who was much improved but still given to bouts of peevishness and screaming fits. Lucy, plunging into the day's work, found the hours too short; two of the girls who came in part time were off sick, and the rest of them were hard put to it to get through the ever-recurring chores. She went home late to find her sisters waiting for her.

'You must give up that job,' declared Imogen. 'It's ridiculous to work yourself to the bone like this. There's no need——'

'But I like my work, and it's useful, even if it isn't important.'

Imogen went red. 'You know Mother would love to have you at home, especially now Pauline and I will be getting married.'

'Well, I am at home each evening, and Mother and Father are often out or away.' She smiled suddenly. 'Don't let's talk about me—tell me if there are any more plans for the weddings.'

Her mother telephoned that evening too; they had discovered more iron pots and tools and now her father intended to travel some miles into the desert to investigate local tales of more finds. 'So we shan't be home for another few weeks, darling. Did you have a good holiday?'

She didn't wait for Lucy to reply. 'Ask Imogen to come to the phone, will you, Lucy? I want to know the exact date of her wedding...'

Both weddings were going to be rather grand affairs, Imogen's first, in July, and Pauline's in September, but the girls were already making lists of guests and wedding presents, and weighing the merits of oyster satin against white crêpe. Lucy, as keen as any girl to wear white satin and orange blossom, began to alter her ideas. Just to slip into a small church and get married without guests or bridesmaids seemed preferable. Perhaps, she thought wistfully, if ever she should marry, she would change her mind. Other girls' weddings weren't the same as one's own.

It was almost the end of the week when she saw William, but not to speak to. She had just stepped off the bus on her way home when the Rolls slid past. Fiona was sitting beside him, and as her eye caught Lucy's she smiled; it wasn't a nice smile, and she made no effort to draw William's notice to Lucy standing there on the pavement. Lucy would have been very surprised if she had. Somehow the little episode made her resolve to marry William quite hopeless, so that when she got home and found Pauline waiting for her with an invitation to join a party of friends for dinner and dancing on the following evening she accepted at once. It was to be quite a grand affair, Pauline told her—a celebration of Cyril's promotion. His sister and brother-in-law would be there, a couple of old friends, and Cyril's unmarried brother. A daunting thought if he was anything like Cyril, reflected Lucy, but an evening out would distract her thoughts from William.

It was a pity that the orphans had been particularly trying all day, so that when she got home an evening out was the last thing she wanted. But a hot bath and a pot of Alice's tea improved her outlook; she dressed with care in the grey dress she had hoped William would have admired, did her hair in a top knot fastened with a glittering bow, eased her feet into her sandals and went downstairs to join Pauline.

'That's nice even if it isn't new,' said Pauline kindly. 'It's a pity Imogen couldn't make it. Cyril will be here in a moment.' She studied Lucy's quiet face. 'Are you working too hard? You're thinner, aren't you, and a bit pale? Never mind, you'll be all the better for an evening out.'

Cyril came then, more self-important than ever, taking Lucy's congratulations as his rightful due before driving them off to the Savoy. 'Bertram will meet us there with the others,' he told them. 'His days are very full now that he has taken silk—he should go far.'

'I'm sure you'll go further,' murmured Pauline dutifully. 'This promotion is marvellous.'

Lucy, sitting in the back seat, watched the smug little nod he gave in answer. She hoped that Bertram would prove to be a different kettle of fish.

He was the counterpart of Cyril—she saw that the moment the party gathered in the foyer, and her heart sank. There was no hope to be got from the old friends either, as they were middle-aged and devoid of conversation, and Cyril's sister was a disheartened doormat, hardly speaking and, when she did, looking around her apologetically as though requesting permission to speak. Lucy, sitting next to Bertram and with the old friend on the other side of her, listened to the one deploring the young people of today and the other giving her a blow by blow account of some dreary lawsuit in which he had apparently shone. She murmured at intervals and ate the food on her plate with pleasure. There hadn't been much time for lunch at the orphanage, and she was hungry, but that proved to be a problem too, for everyone else was pecking at his or her food in a polite way and the old friend began a stern lecture on the evils of rich food and drink. Lucy wondered why he had come since he felt so strongly about it, and would have had a second helping of the delicious chicken à la King only Bertram pushed back his chair and invited her to dance in what she imagined might be his barrister's voice. She got up obediently and everyone else at the table looked up from their discussion about Fine Art and smiled kindly at her. Cyril's smile was particularly benevolent; she was having a treat and he was the donor.

Bertram was an appalling dancer; her feet, already a little painful from the too-tight sandals, became a problem which emptied her head of every thought other than evading his clumsy steps. They lumbered round the dance-floor while he described just how astute he had been in the case of Biggins versus Potts. Lucy, concentrating on her feet, consigned the pair of them to the bottom of the sea and Bertram with them while she nodded and smiled and said, 'Did you really? You must be clever—of course, I don't know a thing about law...' A mistake, for he began to explain it to her. She pinned a smile on her face and winced as he trod rather more heavily on her toes, and just at that moment Dr William Thurloe danced past, Fiona Seymour in his arms. He looked straight at Lucy, half smiling, and she widened her smile for Bertram's benefit and gave William a small, cool nod. A really tremendous urge to evade Bertram's clutches, push Fiona out of the way and dance off with the doctor filled her person with a fierce wave of rage at meeting the pair of them when she least expected to, and when her feet were killing her too. Mercifully the music stopped, and they went back to the table, where she accepted dessert with relief and slid her poor feet out of the sandals.

She had barely had a mouthful of the caramel mousse when there was a general uprising of the men in the party and she looked up to see Fiona and William standing by the table.

'Pauline,' gushed Mrs Seymour, 'I have not yet wished you happy, and I must congratulate Cyril. When is the wedding to be? And I see that Imogen is to marry too. How exciting.' She gave a trill of laughter and looked across at Lucy. 'Don't get left behind, Lucy.'

Lucy smiled sweetly, her eyes glittering greenly. 'There's a proverb about the hare and the tortoise,' she said gently. 'Better still, do you know a writing of John Burroughs? It's called "Waiting".' She recited clearly, '"Serene I fold my hands and wait, Nor care for wind or tide nor sea; I rave no more 'gainst time or fate, For lo! my own shall come to me."'

There was a small outburst of clapping and laughter, and Pauline said, 'Darling, how very apt, and fancy remembering it—you were always quoting poetry when we were at school. I just hope it comes true for you.'

Fiona had been looking uncertain; she had been quite out of her depth, as she had never bothered with poetry and thought it rather silly and a waste of time. She said charmingly, 'Oh, of course it will. I dare say Lucy will surprise us all.'

She smiled around the table and Bertram said quickly, 'I say, would you care to dance? The band is splendid...'

It was the signal for the general movement towards the dance-floor, save for Lucy, searching feverishly under the table with her feet, hunting for her discarded sandals.

'I won't ask you to dance,' said William in her ear. 'Although nothing would give me greater pleasure, I suspect that you have taken your shoes off. Would it not be a better idea to buy sandals which fitted your feet? And stop poking around like that—I'll get them and we can sit here comfortably while you cram your feet back in.'

He's so nice and ordinary, reflected Lucy, watching him bend his great height to forage under the table and put her shoes where her feet could reach them. He had done it without fuss and quickly, waving away a waiter anxious to be of help, and then he pulled out the chair beside her and sat down.

'And are you settling down after your holiday?' he asked.

'Yes, no—I don't know. It's been busy at the orphanage.'

'All the more reason to enjoy this pleasant little evening party,' his voice was silky, 'but I suspect that you are not doing so.' He lifted a finger and spoke to a waiter, then turned to look at her. 'I like that dress—I liked it last time too...'

Lucy blushed. 'Oh, do you? I thought——' She stopped, and started again. 'That is, I thought...' She gave up and sat looking at him for a long moment, watching the slow smile etch his firm mouth. The arrival of the waiter with champagne in an ice-bucket broke the spell.

William said pleasantly, 'I feel that, since we have joined your party for the moment, the least we can do is to drink to our—er—further acquaintance.'

'How nice,' said Lucy inanely. She hoped the band would go on playing for a long time yet.

William crossed one long leg over the other. 'You read poetry? Do you enjoy John Donne?'

'Very much, though sometimes I'm not sure if I understand all his poems, but some lines—they stick in one's head.' She added almost humbly, 'I'm not clever.'

'If by that you mean you can't add up two columns of figures at the same time or use a computer or understand the Stock Market, then no, you're not clever in the accepted terms of the word. On the other hand, you have an understanding of babies and children and animals, and that is a gift beyond mere cleverness. Also you have the gift of holding your tongue when others might regrettably allow theirs to run away with them.'

She said with something of a snap, 'You make me sound like a saint!'

'Heaven forbid! You're a girl with green eyes.' He smiled at her with a certain touch of mockery and got up as the rest of the party returned to the table.

Fiona tucked her arm in his at once. 'William, why didn't you ask Lucy to dance? Have you just been sitting there talking?'

He didn't answer her, only smiled a little and beckoned the waiter to uncork the champagne, and a moment later everyone was talking at once and happily toasting Pauline and Cyril. Presently William and Fiona went back to their table, and Lucy, glancing round with what she hoped was a casual air, saw them dancing again.

Bertram saw her watching them and said enthusiastically, 'I say, what a splendid woman Fiona Seymour is, and a marvellous dancer. She was very interested in the law—a most intelligent woman and a good listener.'

From which remark Lucy deduced that she was neither.

The party broke up soon afterwards, Lucy said goodbye to Cyril's sister and her husband, the old friends and Bertram and got into the car with Cyril and Pauline. She had eased sore feet into her sandals but they still hurt, which made the evening seem even worse than she'd thought it had been. By the time they arrived at the house she was sunk in gloom, for Cyril and Pauline had been discussing Fiona and William, taking it for granted that their engagement would be announced any day now. Lucy retired to bed in a dark mood and cried herself to sleep.

Pauline spent the day with Cyril on Sunday, and Lucy spent the day in the quite nice garden at the back of the house, weeding and digging and hoeing, and in the evening she had a long talk with Fran on the phone. Fran didn't mention William, which was a good thing, for Lucy was not in the mood to unburden herself to anyone who would listen. Indeed, when Alice questioned her about the dinner party she told her that it had been quite nice, but that Cyril's brother was just as prosey as he was. She described the food, the other guests and the splendours of the Savoy Hotel, but she didn't breathe a word about Dr Thurloe, although she longed to do so, and Alice was wise enough not to mention him either.

Lucy went to work on Monday morning cheered by the thought of a hard day's work ahead of her. One of the nurses was on holiday and Sister had days off. While Lucy had been in Holland a few of the older children had been taken to Madame Tussaud's and the trip seemed to have unsettled them, so that Sister had had her hands full for the rest of the week and had put off her free time. Before she had gone off duty on Saturday she had confided in Lucy that she thought she had a heavy cold coming on. 'I must have caught it during that outing, although that was ten days ago now, but it's since then that I've been feeling a bit under the weather. I feel a bit mean taking days off as we're short-staffed, but I really do need a break,' she'd said.

Lucy had assured her that they would manage, and reminded her that the nurse on holiday would be back in a few days' time and everything would be normal again. 'And until then,' she said cheerfully, 'I'm sure we'll cope. You have a good rest.'

Sister, knowing Lucy to be a sensible girl and not given to panicking in an emergency, presently went home.

The orphanage was already well into its day when Lucy got into her white overall, reported to the senior nurse and went to see Miranda. The child was making progress, slow but steady. Lucy fed, bathed and dressed her, gave her some toys to play with and started on the next toddler. There were only six children between one and two years at that time—there were a great many babies, and the vast majority were five-and six-year-olds, who went to the infant school close by. One or two of the toddlers appeared to have colds, Lucy noted, and at lunchtime one of the older ones was brought home from the school feeling poorly.

'Just when we're short-staffed,' said Matron worriedly. 'Thank heaven Sister will be back tomorrow.'

But Sister wasn't back in the morning. When Lucy got to the orphanage the next morning it was to find a harassed Matron; several of the older children were feeling poorly and the nurse who was due back from her holiday that day was still in Greece because of an airline strike. Matron was a level-headed woman, not easily put out. 'If it's flu,' she observed, 'we shall have our hands full.'

'If it would help, I could sleep here until Nurse Swift gets back,' suggested Lucy diffidently. 'And I don't mind working different hours...'

'Bless you, it would be such a help. I'll make up your hours when we are fully staffed again and all the children are better. Sister hopes to be back within a few days—some kind of cold, she thought, or flu.'

'Then if I may I'll go home at lunchtime and fetch a few things,' said Lucy, 'and let our housekeeper know.'

Alice didn't approve when she was told. 'I don't know what your ma would say, Miss Lucy—that nasty flu—you don't want to catch it.'

'Well, I dare say I shan't, Alice. You know I never catch anything. Dr Watts is coming this afternoon to take a look at the children. Will you tell Pauline and Imogen, and if Mother phones tell her I'm quite all right? I dare say I'll be home in a couple of days—it's only until this nurse can get back from Greece and Sister is better. There's a part-time nurse off sick too, and when she's back we shall be back to normal.' With that little bit of information Alice had to be content.

Dr Watts came late that afternoon, examined the sick children and then spent half an hour closeted with Matron and came out of her office looking serious. Lucy, passing the open door, heard him say, 'I'll be in first thing in the morning. We shall have to check every single child and baby, and all the staff. You must warn your staff—you say there's Nurse Swift on holiday? She mustn't come here. And get hold of Sister at once. I may be wrong—I shall be able to tell you if I'm right in the morning.'

Lucy had paused and unashamedly listened. Something serious, she guessed. Measles? Mumps? Just flu?

Whatever it was, Dr Watts, the most phlegmatic of men, sounded concerned. She went on her way with a load of small garments for the washing-machine, and when she got back to the nursery where the babies were she said nothing to the nurse who was there. Matron would tell them, and until then there was plenty of work to keep her busy. More than enough.

Normally one nurse did night duty, knowing that she could call upon Sister or Matron should things get too much for her. Normally the children slept well, and once the babies had been fed and tucked down for the night they slept too until their early morning feed. The nurses who lived in worked in shifts so that there was one on duty at six o'clock each morning to help the nurse on night duty, but it was obvious as evening approached that more than one nurse would be needed for the night.

'Do you suppose,' suggested Matron to Lucy, 'that you could stay up just for tonight? You should be able to get some sleep, only I don't want to leave Nurse on her own. I'll get up if necessary, but with so many children poorly she won't have much time to see to the babies. And there's Miranda...'

Miranda was being difficult; Lucy hadn't been able to spend as much time as usual with her, and she was working herself into a state.

Lucy was tired and her feet ached; she had been padding to and fro all day, but then so had everyone else and she had just come back from holiday.

'Of course I'll stay up, Matron. If I can get Miranda to go to sleep I'll be free for the rest of the night to help out.'

'Good girl. I must confess I shall be glad when Dr Watts comes in the morning. I shall be in the office until

midnight and be up to help with the feeds in the morning.
As soon as the children are seen to for the day you must
go off duty..'

Miranda took a long while to settle and the rest of the
children were unusually restless and wakeful. Only the
babies, once they were fed, slept peacefully. Lucy went
in search of Nurse Stokes and found her taking a six-
year-old boy's temperature. 'It's very high,' she whis-
pered. She looked at the chart Matron had hung up at
the end of his bed. 'It's gone up, too.' And by the
morning, several of the other children were feverish too.
Matron, up and about by six o'clock, studied each ill
child in turn and then telephoned Dr Watts.

He came so quickly that Lucy wondered if he had been
expecting Matron to call him, and after examining the
most poorly of the children he went to the telephone.
Twenty minutes later Lucy looked up from trying to get
one of the small girls to drink and saw Dr Thurloe, in
thin sweater and corduroys, standing in the doorway
talking to Dr Watts. His eyes swept over her without any
sign of seeing her; he needed a shave and his face was
lined with fatigue. She wanted very much to go to him
and put her arms around him and tell him not to worry.
That was about the silliest thing she could do, she told
herself, and applied herself once more to coaxing the
little girl on her lap to drink.

Dr Thurloe was there for a long time, meticulously
examining each child in turn and then going into
Matron's office to talk to Dr Watts and Matron. On his
way out he met Lucy, her arms full of clean baby clothes.
He stopped and gave her a tired smile. 'Matron will be
talking to you all presently,' he told her. 'I'm afraid we
have an outbreak of legionnaires' disease on our hands.

Some of the children must have picked it up when they had their outing while we were in Holland. They'll have to be sent to hospital and there are quite a few suspects. Matron tells me you're living in for the moment.'

Lucy nodded. 'Have you been up all night?'

He rubbed a hand over his unshaven chin. 'Yes. Why do you ask?'

'Well—I just thought it would be nice if you could go home and have a good sleep——'

He gave a shout of laughter. 'Don't waste your pity on me, Lucy!' He stopped abruptly when he saw the look in her face. 'I'm sorry, my dear, but sleep is the last thing I'm thinking of at the moment.' His eyes searched hers. 'You're going to be busy, do you know that? If you would rather go home, say so now. You aren't trained; you are under no professional obligation to stay.' He added, 'I believe that your parents might not like you to remain.'

'Pooh!' said Lucy forcefully. 'They're not here anyway, and I'm quite able to decide these things for myself, thank you. Of course I'm staying. I may not be trained, but I'm another pair of hands.'

He ran a hand through his hair. 'I'm sorry, I've said it all wrong, haven't I? And you must be asleep on your feet.' He bent suddenly and kissed her gently. 'Off you go, and do whatever it was you were doing, and then for heaven's sake go to bed. You look like a small dozy doormouse.'

She was sent to bed presently after a meal and awakened again at teatime, much refreshed, to plunge back into the never-ending round of feeding and cleaning up and bed making. Soon after five o'clock Dr Thurloe came again, this time the image of an eminent specialist in his sober grey suit and snow-white shirt, and he stayed for some time, checking the progress of several suspect cases and then examining the well ones as well. All the suspected cases were together now, and the babies had been moved to the floor above. That evening an agency nurse was to come to look after them during the night, and a second nurse would take her place in the morning, which left everyone else free to look after the toddlers and the older children—no easy task since so many of them were isolated.

Lucy was to go on night duty with another nurse, and, since her nursing skills were basic, she was given the well children to look after with strict instructions to warn someone at once if any of them showed any signs of the illness. The night shouldn't be too busy, a tired Matron had told her. 'Eight children are in hospital,' she'd added. 'Two of them are very ill, and there are another nine suspected cases here. Hopefully they are only suspected, but we shan't know that for a day or two. Nurse Swift will be back tomorrow afternoon, she refuses to stay away, and there is another agency nurse coming part time.'

The toddlers and older children slept in dormitories of six or eight beds, and they normally slept through the night, but their day had been disrupted and they were inclined to be querulous. Miranda, aware that something was wrong, was indulging in screaming fits. It was almost midnight by the time Lucy had the children quiet and settled and was able to sit down under the shaded lamp and con the instructions she had been given. She was interrupted by the soft-footed entry of Dr Thurloe. He looked fresh and well fed and immaculate, which only served to remind her that she was hardly looking her best. She was still tired, and it had seemed a waste of time to do more than brush her hair severely into a french pleat and leave her face unmade-up. All the same, she looked very pretty in the dim light of the shaded lamp.

He said, 'Hello,' softly and went on to ask a string of questions. 'Any trouble with Miranda?' he wanted to know finally.

'Well, she took ages to drop off—things have been a bit different, moving cots and children and so on, and she didn't like that.'

'You slept?'

'Yes, thank you. How are the children who went to hospital?'

'Holding their own, although there are two very ill little girls. Litrik phoned today—he and Fran send you their love.'

'Oh, that's nice. It seems such a long time ago...'

'But still very much alive in my thoughts. Yours too?' He stood looking down at her, smiling a little.

'Well, yes. Do you want to look at the children?'

'A quick round if I may, although I'm pretty sure this lot you've got here are going to be all right.'

'Are there any more cases—outside the orphanage?'

'Several. Don't get up, I'll just stroll round and cast an eye.'

He wandered off, in an out of the dormitories, and then back to where she was sitting. 'Everything quiet. Are you on permanent night duty?'

'I don't know. Nurse Swift will be back tomorrow and there's another agency nurse coming.'

He nodded. 'Matron is a most capable woman. Goodnight, Lucy.'

He had gone as silently as he had come, leaving her to dream. But not for long—a small demanding voice wanting a drink of water brought her back to reality.

As for Dr Thurloe, he left the orphanage, got into his car and drove to Lucy's home. Late though it was, there were lights shining from several downstairs windows. He rang the bell and Imogen opened the door.

She gave him a look of smiling surprise. 'Oh, hello— do come in. Is this a social call? Would you like some coffee? Alice is getting ready for bed, but Pauline and I have been out and are only just back.'

He followed her into the drawing-room and Pauline looked up with a smile. There were fashion magazines all over the floor and a number of pattern books on the table. 'Hello, how nice to see you. As you see, we're busy planning our weddings. Do sit down—have some coffee?'

'Thank you, no. I can't stop. I thought you might like to know that I've seen Lucy at the orphanage. She's doing night duty and coping very well.'

'She's such a sensible girl,' said Imogen. 'Pig-headed about this job of hers, but she really likes it. Alice said there's flu there.'

'Legionnaires' disease, which is a rather more serious matter.'

'It's not catching?' Pauline looked up sharply. 'Lucy isn't ill?'

'No. It isn't transmitted from person to person, only through the air.'

'Oh, good. Seemingly she left a message to say she would stay at the orphanage for a few days. I dare say she'll phone when she wants to come home.'

The doctor said in an expressionless voice, 'Oh, I'm sure she will. It was kind of you to see me at this late hour. Goodnight, I'll see myself out.'

They chorused a goodnight and added vague wishes that they might meet at some future date. Alice was waiting by the door when he reached it.

'Miss Lucy—she's all right, Doctor? She's not working too hard? She won't catch anything?'

He smiled kindly at her. 'She's fine, Alice, working hard, but perfectly all right. I'll keep an eye on her.'

'She's such a dear girl, Doctor.'

'Yes, she is, Alice. Don't worry about her. Has her mother phoned?'

Alice shook her head. 'No. What shall I say?'

'Why, that she is living at the orphanage for a few days because some of the children are ill and they are short-staffed. Mrs Lockitt has no cause to worry.'

Alice stared up at him. 'She never worries about Miss Lucy—only that she doesn't get married.'

'Well, we shall have to do something about that. Goodnight, Alice.'

Alice went back to the kitchen and began to lock up for the night. 'Well, I never did,' she muttered to Mrs Simpkins. 'I wonder if 'e meant what I think 'e did! And 'er sweet on 'im too. And would 'e know that?'

Mrs Simpkins blinked yellow eyes and curled herself into a tidy ball preparatory to a good night's sleep, so that Alice was obliged to answer her own question. 'Course 'e knows,' she told herself, and nodded her head in a satisfied manner.

Lucy, happily unaware of the interest being taken in her future, had no time to speculate about it during the next few days. Even with Nurse Swift and the part-time helpers there was an endless round of chores, and the news that Sister was laid low with legionnaires' disease had cast a gloom over everybody. Dr Thurloe came and went, sometimes with Dr Watts, sometimes alone; one of the suspected cases had turned out to be positive and had been taken to the hospital, and there were still several suspected cases among the older children.

Lucy worked through the nights and sometimes for part of the day too, and she didn't sleep well and began to look rather pale and wan. She had formed the habit of getting up long before she needed to and taking herself for a brisk walk through the dreary streets around the orphanage. It was on her return from one of these unsatisfactory outings that she came face to face with the doctor.

He took her by the shoulders and studied her face. 'Not sleeping? Feel all right? Suffering from a surfeit of orphans?' He didn't wait for her answer. 'Time that you had a day off.'

She said stiffly, 'Thank you, but I don't want one. None of us is having one and we can manage very well.'

He nodded. 'I am sure you can. Fiona asked me to invite you to her birthday party on Saturday...'

A little colour crept into her cheeks. 'How kind. Especially as she doesn't know me very well, but I can't accept. Please thank her from me when you see her. I hope that she has a happy birthday.' She added waspishly, 'They're fun, even when you're getting on a bit...' She gasped. 'Oh, I'm sorry I said that. I—I didn't mean it, she's quite lovely and striking even if she is——' She stopped herself just in time. 'What I mean is you must be very proud of her.'

She fled then, darting past him and down the passage, leaving him smiling and presently laughing.

CHAPTER EIGHT

THE days slipped by, and two more children were taken
to hospital, but the other suspected cases remained well
and the first little patients who had been in hospital for
a week or more were responding well to erythromycin.
All the same, everyone on the staff went round on the
alert for shivering fits, coughs and high temperatures.
Dr Thurloe came and went, and on one occasion Lucy
was summoned to hold Miranda while he checked her
shunt, during which he had little to say other than to
ask a few questions and give some simple instructions.

'Miranda's doing well,' he told Lucy. 'What is needed
shortly is a loving foster parent.' He spoke with pleasant
aloofness, so that Lucy felt very aware of her humble
status and burned with what was misplaced resentment.
She didn't answer him and he looked at her briefly.
'Largely due to you, Lucy,' he added kindly. 'Now, I
wonder if I might talk to Matron for a few minutes.'

The signal for her to carry Miranda back to her cot
and tuck her up for her usual afternoon nap. The moppet
had no wish to do anything of the sort. Kindly, Lucy
sat with Miranda on her lap, carrying on the quiet gossipy
talk which she liked and which soothed her, while Lucy
allowed a small part of her mind to dwell on William.
That she loved him she had no doubt; that she didn't
understand him was very clear to her. One moment he
was a friend, almost more than that, the next he was a

kind, rather distant consultant who spoke to her with great civility and not a trace of friendliness.

She soothed Miranda to sleep at last and went away to feed the smallest of the babies.

The doctor found her ten minutes later. 'Alice asked me to give you these letters,' he observed.

'Alice?' She forgot she was annoyed with him in her surprise.

'I called to let her know how you were. She worries about you.' He smiled faintly. 'So do I.'

'Well, there's no need,' said Lucy tartly. 'I'm not a young girl, you know...'

He put the letters on the cot beside her. 'No, you're not,' he agreed, quite unruffled. 'You're a very pretty young woman, and at the moment, I suspect, a cross one.'

He went away before she could do more than goggle at him.

Two days later, just as things were beginning to quieten down, Miranda began to shiver and cough and run a high temperature.

'But she didn't go with the other children,' cried Lucy, cuddling the unhappy toddler on her lap.

'No, but while you were in Holland—the day you came back, in fact—she was taken out in her pushchair and, as far as I can make out, it was to the same area,' Matron sighed. 'There's no end to it. Dr Thurloe is on his way— she will have to be X-rayed, as she's chesty.'

The doctor, presenting an unshakeable air of confidence, confirmed Matron's fears. 'I'll have her in—she will need an X-ray and careful nursing.' His thoughtful eye studied Lucy, holding the child. 'If you can spare her, Lucy had better come too; Miranda must be kept content and as quiet as possible.' He turned away. 'Fix up an ambulance, will you, Matron? I'll just check those two suspects while I'm here.'

He went away, and so did Matron, leaving Lucy soothing Miranda. She could have done with some soothing herself. No one had asked her if she minded going to the hospital—not that she had the slightest objection, but it would have been nice to have been asked. 'I might just as well have been a chair,' she said indignantly to the moppet grizzling on her lap.

'Nothing—absolutely nothing would convince me that you look like a chair,' said William from the door. 'And if I have taken advantage of your good nature it is because I have a good deal to worry about just at this moment.'

Lucy twisted her head round to look at him. 'Oh, William, I'm sorry, I truly am. And you're tired too. Do you get enough sleep?'

His mouth twitched. 'Why, thank you, Lucy, just about enough. The worst seems to be over—they've traced the source to the water-cooling plant on one of the stores and it's being dealt with. There haven't been any fresh cases for three days. It is unfortunate that our Miranda should fall sick—you'll come to the hospital with her?'

'Yes, of course. Is she very bad?'

'No worse than several others, but we have the added complication of the shunt. Provided we can keep her happy and as comfortable as possible, she should do. I'll start the antibiotic course at once.' He turned to go. 'I'll see you at the City Royal.'

He might be a busy man, but he had found time to arrange for Miranda's admission. At the hospital, Lucy tucked her up in her cot in a glass-walled cubicle in one of the children's wards, and was led away to be shown where she was to sleep. It was a small room adjoining the ward, one of several set apart for mothers of ill children. 'And you can be free from one o'clock until teatime each day,' said the ward sister, a fierce, elderly dragon with a beaky nose and old-fashioned spectacles. 'I shall expect you to look after Miranda during the rest of the day and, if necessary, until she settles for the night. Have you an overall?'

Lucy said yes meekly, and presently unpacked her overnight bag and put away the few essentials she had stuffed it with, then went back to Miranda, who was lying back in her cot. She looked very ill and she was in a furious childish rage. Lucy took down the cot sides and sat her on her lap and talked to her.

She was still murmuring the tale of the Three Bears when Dr Thurloe and Sister came in. 'The child should be in bed,' Sister spoke sharply and Miranda let out an outraged yell.

'You are quite right, Sister,' said William suavely, 'but perhaps in this case it might be best if Miranda were pandered to; you know her case history, do you not? I am anxious that she is kept as quiet as possible until her chest clears. I'd like her X-rayed as soon as you can arrange it.'

He held out a hand and the house doctor, who had slipped in behind him, handed him a form. He filled it in and handed it to Sister. 'There is some consolation in the lungs.' He spoke to the young doctor. 'Keep a sharp eye open, Charles, and let me know if you are worried. Miss Lockitt understands how the shunt works, but check it if you please.'

He smiled at the young man and turned to Sister. 'I know Miranda is in your very good hands, Sister.' He smiled again with great charm and that lady bridled and allowed her severe features to relax.

He turned to go. 'Take a look at the X-rays and let me know, Charles. I'll be at my rooms until six o'clock. Good day to you, Lucy.'

She was tempted to say, 'Good day to you, William,' but instead she allowed a respectful murmur to escape her lips, which caused Sister to cast her a look of limited approval. At least the young woman knew her place.

Miranda gave Lucy no peace for the rest of the day, and twice in the night she was called because Miranda's screams of rage were keeping the other children awake, so that by one o'clock the next day Lucy was more than ready for a few hours' freedom. A quick lunch, she thought, and then bed. Sister had told her sharply that she should take some exercise during the afternoon, but to curl up on her bed and sleep was all she wanted.

She went down the corridor to the lifts. The dining-room was in the basement, three floors down; she would have a hurried snack, she decided, her finger on the button. The lift door opened and William stepped out.

'There you are,' he remarked pleasantly. 'Get that overall off, I'll be outside in five minutes.'

'Why? I'm going to bed . . .'

'No, you're not. Just get out of that thing, never mind how you look. You're coming back with me for lunch and then you can lie in the garden and sleep.'

Her mind fastened on the one important thing in this speech. He didn't care how she looked, which was even further proof of his indifference to her. She said pettishly, 'I don't want to.'

There was no one to see them, and William started to unbutton the nylon garment she was wearing. She had a strong feeling that even if the corridor had been knee-deep in people he would have done the same. He finished the buttons and said, 'Well, take it off, dear, we shall be here all day and I'm hungry.'

The pettishness was giving way to a pleasantly vague feeling that she need not bother about a thing because William would see to everything. She took off the garment, folded it carefully and hung it over her arm. 'My hair,' she said. 'And I want to wash and do my face.'

'And so you shall.' His voice was soothing. He pressed the button, and, when the lift opened its door, pushed her gently into it. The lifts were in a row at the back of the entrance hall, and he walked across to the door, nodding affably to the hall porter as they went, and outside, stowed her tidily into the Rolls, got in beside her and drove away.

'I'm on duty at five o'clock,' said Lucy making a last attempt to be sensible.

'Yes, I know. I'll get you back in good time.' He didn't say any more and she sat back, her head pleasantly empty. If their journey had been any longer she would undoubtedly have gone to sleep, but even with the midday traffic it was brief enough. Urged to alight, she sat up as he got out and opened her door, scooped her out and marched her briskly up to the front door where Trump was already standing.

He greeted her with subdued pleasure, listening gravely while the doctor asked him to fetch Mrs Trump, and returned with that lady with commendable speed.

'One of the bedrooms, I think, Mrs Trump,' advised
the doctor. 'You'll see that Miss Lockitt has all she
needs?'

'Indeed I will, sir. You come with me, miss, there's
ten minutes before lunch and you can take all the time
you want.' With which contradictory remark Mrs Trump
trotted up the stairs with Lucy behind her, swept open
a door in a long, narrow passage facing the stairhead
and bustled into the room beyond, where she pointed
out soap, towels, powders, creams and hairbrushes in
the adjoining bathroom, and then bustled away again,
murmuring that she had just the meal for them both.
'Tired to your deaths,' she declared. 'Our dear doctor
on the go all the time, and you too, I dare say, miss.
Now you just put yourself to rights and then come
downstairs.'

It was surprising what a wash, followed by the making
up of her face and a fierce brushing of her hair, did to
ward off Lucy's tiredness. She gave an appreciative sniff
at the several bottles of toilet water standing on the
dressing-table, cast a quick eye round the charming
room, and went downstairs, wondering as she went if
Fiona used that room. Not to stay in, she told herself
hastily; the doctor, she felt sure, was a man to guard his
reputation sternly. He behaved in a high-handed fashion,
it was true, but she fancied that he had strict ideas...

He came into the hall as she reached it. 'Just time for
a drink, in here.'

The room welcomed her, as did Friday and Robinson,
Thomas and the ginger kitten, curled up in a bright patch
of sunlight by the open french doors. She sat in one of
the comfortable chairs and the sherry went straight to
her head, so that she wished that she could sit there

forever. Not that she was given the chance; ten minutes later, during which time William had carried on a mild conversation about nothing at all, she was invited to have her lunch and crossed the hall to the dining-room. Last time she had been there had been with the other guests sitting round the oval mahogany table; now there were just two places laid, side by side at one end. The table was covered by a damask cloth and there was a vase of lilies of the valley and forget-me-nots at its centre. The heavy silver gleamed and the crystal glasses shone and she wondered if William, even when alone, ate his meals in such splendour.

They had potato soup, its humble name concealing a flavour out of this world, followed by fillets of sole, mangetout peas and little new potatoes, and they finished their lunch with a magnificent apple pie with accompanying clotted cream. 'We'll have coffee here,' said William, 'then you can go into the garden and doze. I've a pile of work to do.'

A remark which brought her down to earth with a rush.

She slept, curled up on a soft mattressed lounger, and would have gone on sleeping for untold hours if the doctor hadn't wakened her a couple of hours later. 'Tea?' he wanted to know. 'There's half an hour or so before you need to go back.'

They had tea in the garden too, at a white-painted table under the copper beech in one corner. It was amazing, she thought, how such a small garden had been made to appear spacious with its small velvet lawn, its flower-beds, full of colour, and the high screen of trees. She accepted another of Mrs Trump's feather-light scones and observed that she could stay just where she was forever. A remark she wished to recall the moment she had uttered it, but since that was impossible she mumbled, 'Well, you know what I mean—it's so very pleasant after the City Royal.'

William agreed lazily and watched the quick colour fade again from her cheeks. 'You will have to stay there for some days,' he pointed out, 'and while you are there I just hope you will come here each afternoon. There's nowhere to go around the hospital, and it would take you too long to go home to Chelsea by bus. I'm free for a couple of hours on most afternoons. The car will be outside at one o'clock and I shall expect you.'

Lucy sat up straight. 'Really? How extremely kind of you, but won't it be inconvenient for you? I mean, don't you want to do things when you're free?'

He said carelessly, 'It will make no difference to me, Lucy. Either I dictate letters or catch up on reports and so on, and you are more than welcome to spend an hour or two in the garden.'

His reply chilled her and she thought about refusing his offer. But he had been quite right, there was nowhere to go around the hospital, and to get home and back by bus would take too long. She said meekly, 'Well, thank you, William, if you're quite sure I'm not being a nuisance.'

He took her back presently, leaving her at the entrance with a brief nod and a laconic, 'One o'clock, tomorrow.'

So each afternoon, she was driven to his home, given lunch and installed in a lounger and told to sleep, to be wakened by the pleasant clatter of teacups, with the doctor sitting nearby, reading a newspaper. She began to depend on these quiet hours; Miranda, while not desperately ill, was proving to be a bad patient, not wanting Lucy out of her sight and waking at night, screaming for her. There was little actual work for Lucy, but the days dragged while she did her best to keep the child happy and quiet.

It was almost a week later, after a splendid lunch at the doctor's house, that she was wakened by a tinkling laugh and, before she opened her eyes, she knew whose laugh it was. There was no sign of the doctor, although Trump was arranging the teatray just so, but a moment later, as she sat up, he came out of the house with Fiona.

Lucy got up and went and sat in a chair, aware that she was untidy and crumpled from her nap, a fact which Fiona turned to her advantage at once. She came across the grass, cool and beautifully turned out and oozing charm. 'Lucy—William has been telling me what a Trojan you have been, you must be exhausted. How I do admire you strong young women, I'm hopeless at illness—too sensitive.' She ran an eye over Lucy's flushed face. 'You poor dear, let us hope that they let you have a holiday when you're free of this child—you certainly need it.'

The doctor stood beside her, listening with an impassive face. He observed quietly, 'It's because Lucy is sensitive that she is so successful at caring for Miranda.' He smiled at Lucy, who didn't smile back; she had no reason to.

He hid a smile. 'Will you stay for tea, Fiona? I shall be taking Lucy back very shortly.'

'In that case I'll wait here for you, William; we can have a nice quiet hour or so here—it is such glorious weather.'

'I'm not coming back,' he told her blandly. 'I shall be at the hospital for the rest of the day, and then at a consultants' meeting.'

Fiona frowned. To sit and gobble her tea with William's eye on his watch was pointless. 'I might as well go.' She sighed wistfully. 'I see so little of you, William...' She frowned again, because that sounded as though they were little more than casual acquaintances, not at all the impression she wanted the silly, untidy girl sitting there to have. She gave one of her tinkling laughs. 'Oh, well, perhaps one evening.' She gave him a smiling, questioning look which wasn't noticed, so that her abrupt, 'Well, goodbye, Lucy. I hope you'll be looking better when we next meet,' was uttered in a snappy voice.

She went back into the house; Lucy could hear her voice, high and plaintive, gradually fading away, and presently William came back and sat down, and she poured their tea and embarked on a pointless conversation until he interrupted her without warning. 'You and Fiona don't like each other.'

She answered carefully, anxious not to upset him, since she thought he was so enamoured of the woman, while her loving heart longed to tell him what a frightful mistake he was making. 'Well, we haven't much in common. She's very attractive, and I should think she would be a most amusing companion and a splendid hostess. She dresses beautifully too.' She stopped then because he was looking at her so strangely. He wasn't smiling, and yet she had the impression that he was amused.

'That's very generous of you, Lucy.'

He smiled with such charm and gentleness that she spoke before she had time to stop herself. 'I'd like you to be happy, William.'

'And you think that Fiona Seymour will give me that happiness?' He got up, took her cup and saucer and pulled her gently to her feet. 'Listen to me carefully. She means nothing to me, never has—just someone to take out to dinner or invite to lunch. As you say, amusing and well dressed,' he paused, 'and empty of all feeling. She never asks me about my work either. It satisfies her that I am successful with sufficient money to live in comfort, and know all the right people. If I were to die tomorrow she would feel regret only because she would be forced to find another man to provide her with the kind of life she considers necessary for her happiness.'

'So why do you take her out?' asked Lucy tartly.

He sighed. 'I have been lonely. I love my work, I have friends enough, but that isn't all. I want a wife and children to come home to.' He bent his head and kissed her gently. 'You, Lucy.'

She stared up at him speechless. 'Me?' A great wave of delight swept over her, so that her breath caught in her throat. 'But would I do? I'm not at all clever, I told you that.'

'You are so anxious to be clever, my dear. You cannot see that a string of letters after your name and a highly paid job are of no consequence at all compared with kindness and patience and being able to listen—so many people have lost the art of listening... So would you consider marrying me, Lucy?'

She wished to throw her arms round his neck, but she forbore from that; he had asked her to be his wife, but he hadn't said that he loved her. Even making allowances for his reserved nature, she reflected, that was something that she thought he could have mentioned.

'I should like to think about it,' she told him in a cool little voice which disguised her bubbling excitement. She added, 'If you don't mind.' Anxious to make things clear, she added, 'You see, I thought you were in love with Fiona.' She frowned. 'Won't she mind?'

He looked all at once remote. 'I cannot see why she should mind—I have never at any time even hinted that I wish to marry her.'

'Oh, well, that's all right, then. All the same, I'd like to think about it.'

Of course she would marry him; her heart had told her that, but she had no intention of allowing him to think she would fall into his lap like an overripe apple. Besides, a little voice at the back of her head reiterated, he hadn't said that he loved her.

'I think I should go back,' she said, and without a word the doctor got up.

'We mustn't allow Sister to wait for you,' he said pleasantly, and swept her back into the house and thence into the car, and drove her back to the City Royal.

There was a message for her on the following day. He had gone to Northern Ireland for a consultation and would be away for two days. And when he came back he pronounced Miranda was out of danger and able to return to the orphanage, so that Lucy didn't see him to speak to. She left the hospital with mixed feelings; had William had a change of heart while he was away, or was he annoyed because she had asked him to wait for an answer? And at least, she told herself indignantly, he could have smiled at her.

She settled Miranda back in her own cot and was summoned to Matron's office. Almost all the children were back at the orphanage, although two of the older ones were still in hospital. Sister was back too, and two new assistants had joined the staff.

'You've earned a few days off,' said Matron kindly. 'Let me see, it is Tuesday—supposing you report for duty next Monday morning? I'm sure you must be anxious to go home for a few days.' She added a few words of thanks and Lucy, immensely cheered at the prospect of the best part of a week at home, stuffed her few odds and ends into her overnight bag and caught a bus for home.

Alice was delighted to see her, and over a pot of tea she told Lucy the news. 'Your ma and pa are on their way 'ome,' she declared. 'I 'ad a phone call from someone saying they were expected back very shortly, though 'e couldn't say when exactly. I've got in extra groceries and told the butcher... Miss Imogen and Miss Pauline will be 'ome for supper, they'll be ever so pleased.' She eyed Lucy narrowly. 'You look peaky, love. What you need is a nice quiet day at 'ome! Just you go and put your things away and I'll get you a nice bite of tea.'

It was nice to be fussed over by the kindly Alice. Lucy ate a splendid tea and then went away to wash her hair and do her nails and attend to her neglected make-up. 'Oh, Alice,' she said, 'it's so nice to be home again.' She smiled at her old friend and then surprised the pair of them by bursting into tears. 'I'm just tired,' said Lucy, between great heaving sobs.

'Course you are, ducks. You'll be right as rain in a couple of days. Worked you too 'ard, they 'ave, at that 'ospital. You just go and 'ave that bath and I'll find a nice drop of sherry for you when you come down.'

The dear soul gave Lucy an encouraging push towards the stairs and went in search of Mr Lockitt's best sherry.

As for Lucy, she lay in a blissfully hot and foamy bath and tried to sort out the niggling thoughts whirling around inside her head; none of them amounted to much, but she knew that she wasn't happy and she should have been. William had asked her to marry him, hadn't he? But without any of the romantic trimmings such an occasion surely warranted. She frowned heavily and got out of the too-hot bath, and presently wandered down to the kitchen to drink the sherry Alice had poured for her. She would have to wait until she saw William again, she decided; there was no use getting worked up about it. Fortified by the sherry, she went back to her room, dressed and did her hair and face, and presented her normal self to her sisters when they came home.

They were pleased to see her, enquiring with vague kindness as to whether she had had a boring time in the hospital and not waiting for an answer. But they were glad that she would be free for a few days.

'I had a cable from Father,' Imogen told her. 'It was sent to the office. He and Mother will be home the day after tomorrow. They want me to get a drinks party together so that they can say hello to everyone at one go. It was all very successful, and they'll probably be going back later in the year. So lucky you're here, Lucy. Will you get drinks and food organised for Saturday? I'll phone everyone—it's short notice, but I'm sure they will all come.'

The evening was spent in making plans for the party, and then, inevitably, more plans, this time for the weddings.

Lucy, who had been looking forward to doing nothing for a few days, found herself immersed in preparing for Saturday evening so that she really had no time to think about William. Of course, he was always at the back of her mind; she thought of him with love and longing and a good deal of doubt. Surely if he loved her enough to want to marry her he would have found the time to phone or scribble a note? But he hadn't said that he loved her, had he? The thought recurred at intervals during the next couple of days, and was never wholly absent even during the bustle and excitement of her parents' return.

Professor and Mrs Lockitt, although glad to be home again, were full of their expedition. It had been a tremendous success and every aspect of it had to be discussed and commented on. It fell to Lucy's lot to help with the unpacking, take loads of clothes to the cleaners, make appointments and make sure that everything was in train for the Saturday evening. Not that she minded—she was glad to be kept busy, and, as her mother pointed out, it made a nice change for her after her little job at the orphanage. Lucy agreed, placidly; no one in the family had understood about her work there, and she had long ago given up talking about it. Alice was the only one she confided in and the only one who really understood. But now there was too much to do to think about the orphanage. Caterers were supplying the food—tiny vol-au-vents filled with salmon mousse, creamed chicken, shrimps chopped with scrambled egg, minute sandwiches and *petit-fours*—but glass and china had to be got from the cupboards, flowers had to be arranged and furniture moved.

On Saturday evening Lucy went to her room to dress, satisfied that everything that needed to be done had been attended to. Two of Alice's nieces were coming in to wait, and Alice would be stationed in the kitchen, dealing with the refilling of plates and making sure that there was plenty of coffee should anyone want it, although that wasn't likely. Lucy showered, and, for no other reason than the fact that William had liked the grey dress, got into it.

Her mother frowned when she saw her in it. 'Darling, surely you've got something else than that grey dress? It's quite pretty, but haven't you worn it rather a lot?' She didn't wait for Lucy to answer, but hurried away to greet the first of the guests.

The big drawing-room and the conservatory beyond were soon full. The Lockitts had a great many friends and several distinguished members of the Archaeological Society had turned up, bent on hearing about the professor's finds. Imogen and Pauline had formed their own circle, leaving Lucy to circulate on her own. She was good at that, even though she was shy with people she didn't know very well, but she put people at their ease, moving from one group to the next, making sure that no one was left on their own. She knew everyone there and stopped to chat from time to time, and it was as she was turning away from old Mrs Winchell that she found Fiona Seymour at her elbow. She had known that she was to be invited, but had been at pains to avoid her. It was silly to feel guilty; William had said that he had no interest in Fiona other than that of an occasional companion for an evening out, and she had believed him, but Fiona didn't know that...

She said, 'Hello, Fiona. I'm glad you could come. It's lovely for Mother and Father to have all their friends here.'

'Well,' drawled Fiona, 'they aren't quite my age-group, but I've always enjoyed a party. A pity William couldn't make it.' She watched the colour creep into Lucy's cheeks. She went on smoothly, 'He's always so busy, bless him—he's been away for a couple of days. Northern Ireland again, you know. Of course, he hates to talk about it.' She watched the look of hurt puzzlement on Lucy's face and at once decided to risk passing on some news of her own invention. 'He's at my place now, but don't tell anyone.' She gave Lucy a conspiratorial smile. 'I'm going back and we'll have a cosy little supper together. The weekend together will do him good. He needs peace and quiet and someone who understands him.'

She watched the effect of her words and was satisfied. For good measure, she added, 'He always comes back to me.' She took a glass of wine from a waitress's tray. 'Will you be a darling and make my excuses to your parents? It's been lovely seeing you again. Still at the orphanage?' And when Lucy nodded dumbly, added lightly, 'William says you're one of the Marthas of this world, and I'm sure you are.'

She patted Lucy's arm and smiled her sweet smile and slid away.

'I can't stand that woman,' declared old Mrs Winchell, tapping Lucy sharply on the shoulder. 'What was she saying to you? You look as though you've just been stabbed in the back.'

Lucy looked at the elderly face staring at her with such shrewd eyes. 'Oh, nothing, Mrs Winchell, nothing that matters at all. Let me get you something to eat...'

Everyone went home presently, and Lucy, with the excuse that she should make sure that everything was cleared away ready for the massive washing up which would have to be done soon, kept herself busy until they sat down to a belated dinner. And, since the talk was all of the expedition and its success, and various discussions about their guests and, once again, the weddings, no one noticed that she was rather quiet.

'Tired, dear?' asked her father eventually. 'You look as though you could do with another holiday. Back to work on Monday?'

He smiled broadly; after four years he still regarded her job as something of a joke.

Lucy wasn't tired, she was numb, and a good thing too for she was unable to think. She replied suitably to her father's gentle teasing and listened to everyone's plans for Sunday. Her sisters would be with their fiancés, and her parents were lunching with friends who lived at Henley.

'I dare say you could come too, darling,' said her mother. 'They would never mind an extra guest.'

If William was back, Lucy's tired brain reminded her, there was just the unlikely chance that he might come to see her, even if it were only to explain... 'I promised I'd have lunch with Joe Walter.'

Her mother looked pleased. 'Oh, good, dear. He's such a nice boy, too and the only young man you know well, really, as I was saying to that elegant Mrs Seymour earlier. We shall be back quite late, I expect; they're sure to ask us to stay for the evening.' She looked at Imogen and Pauline. 'And you two? Will you be back for supper—I must tell Alice...' They told her no and she went on comfortably, 'Oh, well, Alice will give you a meal when you get back, Lucy. You'll be all right, dear?'

Lucy said that yes, of course she would, and when presently she lay in bed she planned her day. Joe was invention, of course. She cast around in her muddled head as to where she might go; there were various aunts and uncles and cousins, but they all lived too far away, and besides, if she went out there was a chance that she might meet William and possibly Fiona with him— something to be avoided at all costs. She decided to stay at home. She could garden and lie in the sun, and Alice could go off to her sister's for the afternoon—no one would know and Alice would never tell. She closed her eyes resolutely, determined not to think about William, but it was almost morning before she slept.

The family dispersed by mid-morning and Lucy went to the kitchen to explain to Alice. 'And, darling Alice, if—just if Dr Thurloe arrives before you leave—but he won't—tell him that I'm having lunch with Joe Walter.'

'If you say so, Miss Lucy, though why you have to tell a parcel of lies to such a nice gentleman is more than I can understand.'

'Thank you, Alice. There's—there's a good reason; perhaps one day I'll tell you. I'm going to stay in the garden, it will be super in the sun with nothing to do. I'll get my lunch, so do go to your sister's as soon as you like. Don't come back until after tea—no one but I shall be here.'

Alice agreed reluctantly and presently the house was quiet. Lucy, in an old cotton dress, made coffee and took it out into the garden with the Sunday papers. There was a lot of day ahead of her, but if she read all of the papers properly it would take her until it was time for her to get her lunch. She had been reading for half an hour when the front door knocker was thumped. She shot out of her chair and went quietly into the house, and even more quietly upstairs, to peep out of a bedroom window which faced the street. William's car was outside. He didn't go away for several minutes, and she watched him with longing eyes as he got into the car. He drove away without looking about him, and she went back into the garden. The phone rang twice after that, but she let it ring, sitting with her hands clenched together and her feet boring into the ground to stop her from going to answer it.

The day dragged. She made a sandwich for her lunch, and welcomed four o'clock when she could have a pot of tea. And soon after that Alice came back, fussing because Lucy hadn't had a proper meal. She set about getting one as soon as she had taken off her hat and coat, and Lucy, tired of her own unhappy company, sat at the kitchen table with Mrs Simpkins on her knee and listened to Alice's soothing voice telling of her day. The thump of the knocker took them both by surprise. Lucy got up and went to the door. 'I'm going upstairs. Alice, if it's him tell him I went to lunch with young Mr Walter and I'm not back yet. Quick, Alice, and then perhaps he'll go away.'

She whisked herself upstairs, and Alice went to the door to confront a grim-faced doctor. He heard her out in silence. 'Thank you, Alice,' was all he said, and he went back to his car and drove away.

'What did he say?' asked Lucy, back in the kitchen.

'Just, thank you, Alice. He looked as though he was in a fine temper.'

Which he was. He had returned home very early that morning intent on seeing Lucy. Even Fiona, phoning to see if he was back and with some story about Lucy and young Walter tripping off her tongue, hadn't stopped him. He had been puzzled and then angry when he'd found no one at home, and when at last Alice had answered the door his rage, seldom in evidence, had threatened to choke him. Fiona would have been delighted if she had known the havoc her tissue of lies had wrought.

CHAPTER NINE

MONDAY morning began badly. Lucy overslept because she had lain awake for a good part of the night, unhappy thoughts running round her woolly head and none of them making sense. She missed her usual bus, too, so that she arrived late at the orphanage, with almost no breakfast inside her and a headache. Worse was to follow. As she sat with Miranda on her knee, patiently spooning porridge into the small, unwilling mouth, Matron joined her. Lucy wished her good morning and wondered why that lady looked ill at ease. Because she herself had been ten minutes late? It seemed unlikely, especially as she had explained to Sister about missing the bus. Matron sat down on the only other chair. 'We must have a talk,' she began briskly. 'The Board of Governors have been looking into the administration of the orphanage and have decided to make one or two changes. In short, one full-time member of the staff or two part-time members must be made redundant. I'm more than sorry that it must be you, Lucy—you have been such a good worker here and done so much, but, you see, the two part-time both need the money and, if you will forgive me for saying so, you don't. One has an invalid mother and the other is quite on her own and lives on her wages.'

She paused. Lucy inserted another spoonful of porridge with a gentle cluck of encouragement. 'I quite understand, Matron. I shall be awfully sorry to go, as

I've loved working here, but it's quite true, I don't need the money.' She kept her voice quiet and steady with an effort. 'I would be glad to work here as a voluntary worker...'

'Yes, I'm sure you would, and I would have been so glad to agree to that, but the board emphasised that only a certain number may work here, paid or unpaid.' Matron frowned, 'I can't see why—something to do with reorganisation, I believe. I can promise you that if this can be altered I will let you know at once.'

She got up, looking relieved. 'If you would just work this week out? And I promise you a splendid reference. Believe me, I did my best to persuade the governors, but they were adamant.'

On her way to the door she stopped and came back again. 'I almost forgot to tell you a splendid piece of news. Miranda is to be adopted, by a charming young couple—he's a curate here in London, and they are unable to have children of their own. They have had Miranda for odd days—while you were in Holland—and now she is well again they will come each day so that she gets used to them. She's very happy with them, and she will be with them as much as possible until she actually goes to live with them.'

'Oh, I'm so glad. She'll be happy to have a mum and dad, and she's so much better.' Lucy meant every word of it.

'Largely thanks to you, Lucy.'

It was fortunate that there was precious little time to sit around and mope; it wasn't until she got home that evening that Lucy allowed her thoughts to turn to the future. And even then she was thwarted, since both Imogen and Pauline were at home for the evening and, as was to be expected, they and her mother plunged into talk of the weddings, her father having prudently retired to his study. Lucy, agreeing with her usual calm to everything which was asked of her, consigned her future and William to the back of her head and shut the door on them. Time enough to think things over calmly when the shock of it had died down.

But it didn't; if anything, it got worse. She carried the hurt of it around with her and no one knew except Alice, who, quick to see that Lucy was worrying about something, winkled it out of her one evening when there was no one else at home. Even to her Lucy couldn't bring herself to talk about William, and at the moment she had no idea what she was going to do about him. She supposed that he had been feeling lonely without Fiona and got carried away, and she had hardly discouraged him, and, after all, there was nothing definite, for Lucy hadn't said that she would marry him. All the same, it seemed strange to her that he hadn't written or asked to see her and explain. True, he had called on the Sunday, but even from the glimpse she had had of him from the window he had looked to be in a towering rage. He probably felt a fool. The one thought that consoled her was that she had never even hinted that she loved him. And as for him, well, everyone, she told herself, could have a change of heart. He might, just for a moment, have thought she would make a good wife for him, and for all she knew he might have been unhappy about Fiona...

The week dragged to a close and she went to the orphanage for the last time, and at the end of the day bade Miranda and her small companions goodbye in a cheerful way, and in the same cheerful fashion took her farewell of the rest of the staff there, and, last of all, Matron. Not once did she complain at leaving, but assured everyone who asked that she intended taking a holiday and then looking for a similar job. 'But this time I think I'll go further afield,' she told them. 'I rather like the idea of Scotland.'

Matron looked at her with relief because she hadn't made a fuss. 'Well, remember that I will give you a splendid reference, Lucy.' They clustered round the entrance and she turned and waved when she got to the corner of the street.

It was a Friday evening and the bus queues were long, so she got home later than usual. Since everyone was in the drawing-room, it seemed as good a time as any to tell them. She hadn't expected sympathy, for none of them had ever taken her job seriously, and they offered none.

'Hard luck, darling!' her mother exclaimed. 'But how providential, now you will be at home to help me with the wedding arrangements.'

Pauline chimed in, 'It wasn't worth much, anyway, Lucy—one of those dead-end jobs that get you nowhere.

Imogen added, 'You'll be far more useful at home.'

Lucy bit back an answer to that; to stay home and do the flowers and write her mother's letters inviting friends and accepting their invitations seemed unimportant compared to caring for the daily needs of small orphans, but there was no point in arguing the matter. With a heavy heart and a docile manner she set herself to the trivial tasks her mother handed over to her. That she became a little pale and quiet over the next week or two went unnoticed, except by the faithful Alice, who went around her kitchen muttering to herself and breathing down fire upon the heads of those who had made Lucy unhappy. She even remarked upon Lucy's quietness to Mrs Lockitt, who looked surprised.

'Oh, I hadn't noticed, Alice. She's always been the quiet one, you know that. Anyway, she will be going to the reception in honour of her father next week; that should cheer her up.'

The reception was at Claridge's Hotel, a rather grand affair, and Mrs Lockitt had spent a good deal of time and thought on her dress. So had Imogen and Pauline, and they in their turn persuaded Lucy to get herself a new dress for the occasion. 'Something really striking,' they begged her, and sighed loudly when she showed them the soft grey chiffon dress she intended to wear. It was, in fact, quite charming and suited her, but it had no pretensions to high fashion, and they pointed out that no one was going to look twice at her if she wore it. Lucy forbore from telling them that she had no wish for anyone to look even once at her, and only filial duty was the reason for her going to the reception anyway.

All the same, they had to admit that when she joined them, ready to leave the house, she looked charming in a gentle sort of way.

An opinion echoed by Dr Thurloe, catching sight of her standing with a group of acquaintances before the speeches began. He excused himself from the friends he was talking to and edged his way towards her. Despite his size and bulk, he was a quiet man; she had no notion that he was there beside her until he spoke quietly into her ear.

'You and I have to talk, Lucy.' His voice was pleasant, but there was a hint of steel in it which she was quick to hear.

'Why?' she asked baldly.

'Don't waste time being silly.' He smiled down at her and her heart turned over. 'How very nice you look, like a very beautiful grey mouse.'

'I don't think we have anything to say to each other.' She smiled brilliantly at an acquaintance and waved to him. A third party might be a good idea. William was being charming and it was going to her head. The acquaintance waved back and started to inch towards them, then caught William's eye and inched away again.

'Now, before we have to listen to the speeches—where have you been? On holiday? Ill?'

She said quite fiercely, 'You know quite well that I've been given the sack. They call it being made redundant, and, since you're on the Board of Governors and agreed to it, it's silly to pretend you know nothing about it.'

He said calmly, 'Well, I don't. I wasn't at the last meeting, I gave my vote to someone else to deal with. How did you know I was a governor?'

'I had a letter saying how sorry they were.' Lucy smouldered. 'Bah—they couldn't care less ... and there was your name with all the other VIPs who run the orphanage.' She added thoughtfully, 'You do have an awful lot of letters after your name.'

'Yes, well, that's beside the point. We have to talk—can't we leave here and go somewhere quiet?'

She had become dangerously close to forgetting Fiona. 'There's nothing to talk about,' she said in a cold voice.

He stared at her downbent head. 'Perhaps not now.' He took her hand in his and looked at it. 'No ring?' he asked blandly.

Her green eyes flashed. 'I'm not getting married yet,' she told him sweetly, and turned tail and lost herself in the fashionable crowd around them.

She had made the remark for no reason at all other than to annoy him; it was a pity that it did nothing to clear up their misunderstanding. For the rest of that evening William made no attempt to seek her out again, although he took care to know just where she was and who she was with. It puzzled him that young Joe Walter wasn't there at her elbow, and, for her part, Lucy, chatting with her parents' friends and some younger ones of her own, was puzzled too. Where, she wondered, was Fiona? She cast any number of casual glances around the elegant reception, but there was no sign of her. It seemed strange that she was absent, for she was to be met at almost all the local social gatherings. Perhaps she was ill...

She had in fact, not been invited, and had done her best to persuade William not to go without her, but since she had been unable to see him her arguments on the telephone had fallen very flat. As she had put down the phone she had reflected that he had sounded both cool and casual. Perhaps it was time she gave up her efforts to attract him and looked around for someone else. There had been that American she had met a couple of weeks ago—a poor second to William when it came to looks, but certainly wealthier. William, she had to admit, had been singularly hard to captivate.

It was a pity that Lucy knew none of that, circulating in a very proper fashion, listening to what was said to her and not really hearing a word, although she looked deeply interested and said 'Really?' and 'Oh?' and 'How interesting!' just when she should, so that people told

each other afterwards that she was by far the nicest of
the Lockitt girls, even if the other two were outstand-
ingly clever.

William, watching her without appearing to do so,
found her enchanting, and was quite unable to believe
that she and Joe Walter were intending to marry. He was
prepared to wager every penny he possessed that she was
the last girl in the world to behave as she was behaving
now. It was a pity that he was engaged to give a series
of lectures in Leiden at the medical school and would
be going there early the next day, but he was a patient
man and he could wait for someone he wanted more at
the moment than anything else in the world. That there
was something wrong somewhere was obvious, and possibly ten minutes' talk would have put it right, only Lucy,
usually so malleable and gentle, was in no mood to talk,
and matters would only be made worse. He waited until
Professor Lockitt, as the guest of honour, had made his
farewells and left with his family before he went home
himself.

He didn't go to bed at once, but went to his study and
wrote a note to Lucy, addressed the envelope and sealed
it, and on his way to bed asked Trump to post it in the
morning.

He left the house early the next morning, driving
himself down to Dover to take the hovercraft.

Fiona Seymour rang his doorbell several hours later.
She thought it unlikely that he would be at home, but
she would have one more try before she gave him up for
the American, and, being a determined woman, she intended tracking him down and giving him a last chance
to fall for her. Being also a conceited woman, it didn't
enter her head that his interest in her had been both

passing and very superficial. She intended to weep a little to arouse his pity... Trump opened the door and bade her a polite but guarded good morning. He didn't like her, but no feelings showed upon his face. He listened gravely to her request to see the doctor and informed her with inward glee that he was away from home.

'Where?' she asked, and added, 'I dare say he told me, but I must have forgotten.'

'Abroad, madam, but I have no forwarding address. He will be travelling.'

She pushed past him. 'Then I'll leave a note.' She waited while he shut the door, her eyes taking in with regret the delightful furnishings in the hall which could have been hers... The envelope on the console-table caught her eye and she edged nearer so that she could see the address. And what, she wondered, would he have to say to Lucy Lockitt? She had been sure that he had believed her when she had told him that the wretched girl and Joe Walter were on the point of getting engaged. She went past Trump into the drawing-room, where he provided her with paper and pen and drew up a chair to the davenport in one corner of the room, and she composed a letter she had no intention of leaving for William and pondered the best way to take the envelope as she left the house.

It was easy enough as it turned out; telling Trump that she would take her letter with her in the hope of hearing of the doctor's whereabouts from one of his friends, she went back into the hall and, as he turned to open the door, slipped the envelope down the front of her dress. Once outside, she hurried away as fast as she dared just in case he should notice that it had gone. Providentially a bus drew up at a stop a few yards from the end of

Strand on the Green and, although she did dislike public transport, Fiona jumped on and was borne rapidly away. Fortunately for her, because Trump, closing the door behind her, had swept a sharp eye round the hall just to make sure that everything was as it should be, and had seen at once that the letter had gone. There was no one in sight when he opened the door, so he closed it without haste and went thoughtfully to the kitchen where he conferred with Mrs Trump.

Fiona got off the bus within a few minutes, walked the short distance to her flat and, once there, opened William's letter. Fury at its contents turned her face ugly, but when she had read it a second time a look of cunning triumph took its place. Even if she had lost all hope of charming William into marriage, she could make sure that Lucy Lockitt didn't get him. But she had to have an excuse... She thought for a moment, and then put the letter in her handbag and went out on to the street and took a taxi to the end of the road where Lucy lived. She knew exactly what she was going to say and rang the bell with confidence.

Alice answered the door.

'Oh, good morning—Alice, isn't it? Is Miss Lucy in? Could I see her for a few minutes—just something I have to return.'

Alice admitted her. Lucy was at home, although no one else was, and the good soul, even though she disliked Mrs Seymour, had no reason not to let her in. She showed her into the drawing-room and went in search of Lucy, who was turning out an attic cupboard.

'Oh, bother,' said Lucy, well aware that she was dusty and a bit untidy. All the same, she went downstairs and into the drawing-room to bid Fiona good morning and ask her to sit down. 'Perhaps you would like coffee?' she asked politely.

Fiona shook her head. 'Sweet of you, but I'm on my way to my dressmaker—I shall need lots of new clothes...' She looked arch and Lucy wondered why. She opened her bag and took out something wrapped in tissue paper. 'William found this at the reception yesterday; he felt sure it was yours and he asked me to let you have it. He's gone abroad for a few days.'

Lucy took the packet and unwrapped it slowly. There was a brooch inside, but it wasn't hers. 'He's mistaken, it isn't mine. Perhaps you should take it to the police.'

'Oh, my dear—I'm so sorry to bother you, I wonder why he thought it was yours?' She gave her tinkling laugh. 'We had so much to talk about that it never entered my head to make sure he was right. And now actually I'm so happy and thrilled that I'm scarcely able to hold a sensible thought in my head. You would never know that he was such a romantic man, would you? But this morning I found such a charming letter when I opened my post.' She gave an angelic smile. 'I'm so excited that I must tell someone...' She opened her handbag and took out the letter. 'Poetry, my dear, can you beat that? He writes, ''My dear, darling, do you know your Wordsworth? The bit that goes, 'The past unsighed for, and the future sure'? That's how I feel about you, and I believe you feel it too. When I return we will talk——'''

'I don't think you should be telling me this,' said Lucy in a steady, expressionless voice, 'and I'd rather not hear it. I hope you will both be very happy.'

'What a sweet creature you are,' said Fiona gushingly. 'So understanding, especially as you were growing rather fond of him yourself.'

'William is a very nice person; I think there are a great many people who are fond of him.' Lucy got up. 'Do find the owner of that brooch, she must be so worried.' She went to the door and stood by it, smiling although it was an effort to do so. 'I hope you won't be late for your dressmaker.'

She shut the street door on Mrs Seymour and stood leaning against it, the tears pouring down her cheeks. Things had gone wrong between her and William, but she had still nurtured the hope that they would be put right. Now there was no hope of that. She had been a fool—she should have said yes when he had first suggested marrying her, but since she hadn't, and it didn't seem to have worried him overmuch, she had to conclude that it had been the spur of the moment—just an impulse. Perhaps Fiona had quarrelled with him and he'd wanted to annoy her.

Alice came from the kitchen, offered a large handkerchief and led her back to sit by the kitchen table. 'Now, you just tell me all about it, Miss Lucy. That woman—making mischief, I'll be bound...'

So Lucy told her, and it was a great relief to talk to someone about it, for she felt Alice was the only person who would understand—William would have understood, but telling him, even if she were able, would have made no sense at all.

She drank two cups of tea, listening to kind Alice's comforting clucks and wondering what she should do. Pack a bag and go away on a long visit to one or other of her aunts and uncles living in a variety of rural retreats around the country? Stay and pretend nothing had happened? Do something really drastic like joining the ATS? A notion nipped in the bud by an urgent peal on the door bell.

'Who's that?' she asked. 'Don't let them in, Alice; say there's no one here.'

Alice opened the door to a dignified but agitated Mr Trump. 'I've some urgent news for Miss Lucy, Alice. It's most important.'

'She said not to let anyone in.'

'Tell her it concerns herself and Dr Thurloe.'

Alice opened the door wide. 'Never mind me asking, you come on in.'

He followed her into the kitchen and Lucy, seeing who it was, frowned and then said, 'Trump, good morning. Is something the matter? Can we help?'

'Well, yes and no, miss. There's something I must tell you . . .'

He related the morning's happenings, not leaving out a single detail. 'So you see, miss, Mrs Seymour has the letter which was addressed to you, though I'm sure I don't know why she took it.'

Lucy's face, puffy and red with weeping, had taken on an instant prettiness. 'For me? That letter? She pretended it was for her—she read me some of it.' She smiled at the memory of it. 'Oh, Trump, I can never thank you enough for being so prompt. I know exactly what I must do.' She beamed at him. 'Do sit down and have a glass of beer and tell me where the doctor is.'

He accepted a chair and the beer with a grave inclination of his head. 'As to that, miss, I cannot say exactly. But I was told that he would be in Leiden in Holland for the rest of this week. I believe he is to give a series of lectures there. Presumably the authorities there would know.'

Lucy nodded slowly. 'Better still, those friends I stayed with; they know him well. I'll go there first and then I'll go to Leiden.'

'All that way, Miss Lucy, and supposing you don't find him?'

Lucy smiled radiantly at them both. 'Oh, but I shall,' she assured them. 'Thank you very much for coming, Trump. You have no idea what this means.'

Trump, who had a very good idea, smiled at her in a fatherly fashion. 'I'll be off, then, miss.' He paused. 'How will you go to Holland?'

'Catch a plane.' She glanced at the clock. 'I'll try and get a flight this afternoon.'

'In which case, miss, I'm sure the doctor would wish me to drive you to the airport. If you would be good enough to telephone me when you have made your arrangements I will return here with the car.'

'Not the Rolls?'

'We have a second car, miss, a small Daimler.'

'Well, thank you, Trump, that would be lovely. I'll ring you as soon as I know when I can go.'

On the afternoon flight to Schiphol, crammed between a stout lady who couldn't keep still and a gentleman who coughed a great deal and swallowed pills every ten minutes or so, Lucy took time to reflect upon her extraordinary behaviour. She had booked a seat on the plane, packed an overnight bag, changed into a thin jersey dress and jacket, primed Alice and left a note for her parents. They would possibly be quite bewildered, but not unduly worried; they travelled so extensively themselves that her unexpected trip to Holland would leave them only mildly surprised. Schiphol lay beneath her and she still had no idea what she would do. It had seemed vital to see William at once, but now she was actually in Holland she wasn't quite sure how to set about it. Fran might be able to help. She took the airport bus into Amsterdam and then a taxi to the station and caught a train to Utrecht. There she found a taxi to drive her out to Litrik's home. It was early evening by then, and the house, tranquil in the midst of its lovely gardens, seemed to welcome her. She rang the bell, suddenly feeling foolish.

Trugg opened the door and, to her everlasting relief, welcomed her with a smile and a total lack of surprise. 'A pleasure to see you again, Miss Lockitt. I'll fetch mevrouw...'

Fran was already running down the staircase. 'Lucy, how lovely! You've come to stay? I do hope so.' She tucked her arm in Lucy's. 'Come into the drawing-room, and, Trugg, please ask Mrs Trugg to make sure that the room Miss Lockitt had when she was here is quite ready for her.'

She opened the drawing-room door and urged Lucy into the room. 'Litrik, look who is here. Isn't it great?'

Litrik was on the floor, building a brick castle for his firstborn. He got to his feet, and Lucy, looking anxiously at his face, could see nothing but pleasure at the sight of her.

'I feel awful coming like this,' she began, 'but I—I must see William, and Trump doesn't know where he is. At least, he said he was in Leiden, but he doesn't know just where.'

'Then you've come to the right place, and very sensible of you,' said Litrik kindly. 'William is staying with us, only unfortunately he went to Groningen this morning and won't be back until tomorrow afternoon or evening.'

'That's in the north, isn't it? I could catch a train...'

'Not this evening, my dear. It's quite a long journey— a hundred and thirty miles, two and a half hours' run— and what would you do when you got there?' He caught Fran's eye and smiled faintly. 'Fran has a Mini; I'm sure she won't mind if you borrow it and drive up in the morning.'

'Oh, that would be simply marvellous. You wouldn't mind really?'

'Not in the least, but upon reflection I think it might be a better idea if Trugg were to drive you, then he can bring the Mini back. You will, of course, come back with William.'

Lucy's eyes glowed like emeralds. 'Oh, will I? You won't tell him I'm here? He might not want——'

'Not a word shall be said. Darling, take Lucy up to her room and then we'll have a drink and hear all her news.'

They didn't ask her to explain why she had come. They talked about her parents and her sisters and the children, and listened with sympathy when she told them that she had left the orphanage, never betraying the fact that they had heard it all already from William. Presently they had dinner and, after another hour or so of undemanding talk, Lucy went to bed. She had had every intention of rehearsing exactly what she would say to William when she saw him, but she went to sleep instead.

Driven by a dignified Trugg, she left very soon after breakfast. 'Trugg will bring the Mini back,' said Fran, 'because of course, William will bring you back with him. I'm not sure, but I think he said that he had a lecture in the morning and then intended coming back here. Trugg will take you to the university buildings and see you safely inside. William is lecturing there in the big hall.' She embraced her friend with the remark that she would expect them back for dinner that evening, but earlier if they could manage it. Her matter-of-fact acceptance of Lucy's sudden appearance did much to steady the latter's nerves, which by now were jangling. The drive up to Groningen with the staid but friendly Trugg did much to steady her, and when they reached the university buildings she bade him goodbye and got out of the car without hesitation, although the sight of him driving away considerably lessened her resolution. All the same, she walked boldly through the great doors into the entrance hall, a dark, forbidding expanse of marble floor and dim walls, hung with portraits which looked even darker, and ringed around by busts of long-dead and learned men, each atop his pedestal. A little daunted, she looked around her and saw William at the bottom of the great stone staircase, talking to two elderly men. He looked stern and remote and, as always, faultlessly dressed, but she had no intention of letting any of these intimidate her and started across the marble space between them. She was a third of the way when he saw her, said something to his companions and came to meet her. If he was surprised or pleased there was nothing on his face to show it, but she was past caring about that. She fetched up in front of him and all her well rehearsed speeches flew out of her head. 'I had to come,' she told him breathlessly. 'It was that bit from Wordsworth, you know—''The past unsighed for, and the future sure,'' When she read it, I knew I'd have to tell you.'

William took her two hands in his; he saw that his long-held patience would have to be held for a little longer.

'Tell me about it, my darling,' he said, in the quiet soothing voice in which he spoke to his small, scared patients.

Lucy lifted her face, glowing with love and trust, to his. 'She came to see me yesterday morning—she said you asked her to, that you had found a brooch at the reception and that it was mine and you had asked her to return it. It wasn't until later that I knew that that was an excuse.' She frowned. 'I never wear brooches...'

She paused long enough for the doctor to ask gently, 'Fiona?'

She nodded. 'She saw your letter to me at your house—the one with the Wordsworth in it.' She smiled radiantly for a moment. 'She took it while Trump wasn't looking and then came to see me. She said it was from you to her...' She stared up at his calm face and a tear trickled down her cheek. 'I wanted to die.'

The doctor took a very white handkerchief from his pocket and wiped away the tear, and she went on, 'Then Trump came and told me, so I knew.' She drew a long gulping breath and said uncertainly, 'I came as quickly as I could.'

The hall had filled quite a lot as they had been standing there; students in their variety of coloured caps, learned professors with bald heads, a sprinkling of ordinary looking people, looking rather out of place, all milling around the pair of them just as though they weren't there.

Lucy hadn't even seen them, and the doctor ignored them. 'One small point, my darling—this nonsense about you and Joe Walter...'

She remembered his remark about her ringless hand. 'Oh, did she tell you...? She wanted you to think that Joe and I...so, she could marry you.'

'Er—perhaps I might point out that I have never at any time wished to marry her.' He was still holding her hands tightly. 'The only person I want to marry is you, my dear heart, and I knew that the moment I saw you at the clinic.'

'So did I, only I didn't know it till later on,' said Lucy obscurely.

He let go of her hands, put his hand under her arm and started making his way through the throng.

'Where are we going?'

He didn't answer her, but turned into a narrow dark passage and opened a door. The room was even darker than the entrance hall, a gloomy mixture of dark green curtains and heavy leather furniture.

He pushed her in in front of him and closed the door. 'The consultants' room,' he told her, 'but, as you can imagine, no one comes here unless there's a meeting.'

He grinned suddenly, and she saw with satisfaction that he was going to be fun to live with; under that sombre grey suit was a man who would be a delightful husband. She asked, knowing the answer, 'Why have we come here?'

He took her in his arms and drew her close. 'Because I want to tell you that I love you more than anything or anyone in this world, and, when I've made that quite clear, I'm going to kiss you, both of which I prefer to do in privacy.'

She held him off for a mere moment. 'William, do you think we could be married before Pauline and Imogen? Would you mind?'

He kissed her thoroughly before he answered. 'My dearest love, not only do I not mind, but I insist upon it. A special licence and a quiet wedding within the next week or two.'

An entirely satisfactory answer, reflected Lucy. She said meekly, 'Just as you say, William,' and lifted her face to his.

Coming soon
to an easy chair near you.

FIRST CLASS is Harlequin's armchair travel plan for the incurably romantic. You'll visit a different dreamy destination every month from January through December without ever packing a bag. No jet lag, no expensive air fares and *no* lost luggage. Just First Class Harlequin Romance reading, featuring exotic settings from Tasmania to Thailand, from Egypt to Australia, and more.

FIRST CLASS romantic excursions guaranteed! Start your world tour in January. Look for the special **FIRST CLASS** destination on selected Harlequin Romance titles—there's a new one every month.

NEXT DESTINATION:
AUSTRALIA

 Harlequin Books

JTR3

This February,
Harlequin helps you
celebrate the most
romantic day of the
year with

Valentine

my

_____ *1991*

Katherine Arthur
Debbie Macomber
Leigh Michaels
Peggy Nicholson

A collection of four tender
love stories written by
celebrated Harlequin
authors.

Available wherever Harlequin books are sold.

VAL

Take 4 bestselling love stories FREE

Plus get a FREE surprise gift!

Special Limited-time Offer

Harlequin Reader Service®

Mail to
In the U.S.
3010 Walden Avenue
P.O. Box 1867
Buffalo, N.Y. 14269-1867

In Canada
P.O. Box 609
Fort Erie, Ontario
L2A 5X3

YES! Please send me 4 free Harlequin Romance® novels and my free surprise gift. Then send me 6 brand-new novels every month, which I will receive months before they appear in bookstores. Bill me at the low price of $2.24* each—a savings of 26¢ apiece off cover prices. There are no shipping, handling or other hidden costs. I understand that accepting the books and gift places me under no obligation ever to buy any books. I can always return a shipment and cancel at any time. Even if I never buy another book from Harlequin, the 4 free books and the surprise gift are mine to keep forever.

*Offer slightly different in Canada—$2.24 per book plus 69¢ per shipment for delivery.

Sales tax applicable in N.Y. Canadian residents add applicable federal and provincial sales tax.

116 BPA FAWF (US)   316 BPA WAV2 (CAN)

Name _____ (PLEASE PRINT)

Address _____ Apt. No. _____

City _____ State/Prov. _____ Zip/Postal Code _____

This offer is limited to one order per household and not valid to present Harlequin Romance® subscribers. Terms and prices are subject to change.

ROM-BPADR   © 1990 Harlequin Enterprises Limited